What people are saying about
DEATH IN THE FLOWERY KINGDOM:

I am a dyed-in-the-wool aficionado of author Steven M. Roth and his brilliant detective novels. I was referred to Mr. Roth's first published novel, "Mandarin Yellow," and its fascinating detective hero, Socrates Cheng, by a literary critic.

Mr. Cheng is a mixture of two dynamic and ancient cultures, Chinese and Greek. Cheng blends this cultural background into a relentless search for a murderer. Socrates Cheng continues his search for murderers in Steve Roth's second and third novels, "The Mourning Woman" and "The Counterfeit Twin."

Mr. Roth continued his novel publishing career with two more novels focusing upon a truly remarkable former US Navy Seal personality, Trace Austin. "No Place to Hide" and "No Safe Place" kept me on the edge of my chair. Meticulous research and excellent writing are hallmarks of Mr. Roth's style.

Steve Roth turned the tables on me by taking his readers to Shanghai, China, year 1935, via "Death in the Flowery Kingdom." We are introduced to another fascinating old school, Chinese Inspector Detective Sun-Jin. The reader is immersed into several clashing Chinese cultures. Our hero detective represents Confucius and is relentless in finding the killer of Shanghai's "Sporting Houses." (Red Light District) I detected early-on that there may be a powerful force behind the murders to accomplish a complicated business objective. Shanghai is divided into three zones with each having it own Police Force and governmental structure. In spite of his boss' and council's order to "cease and desist" his investigation, Sun-Jin continues the investigation on his own. There is a sad sub-plot with a classy Russian lady that could be the life partner of Sun-Jin's dreams. Regretfully, this lovely Russian lady falls victim to the killer of Shanghai's prostitutes. Of course, the murders are solved via a surprise ending.

I am impressed with author Steven Roth's meticulous research and well-crafted descriptions. I could place myself on the streets of Shanghai as the author forms engrossing word pictures in his description of Shanghai in the 1930s. Mr. Roth's clear writing style helps the reader negotiate the twists and turns of the compelling plots and sub-plots of every one of his brilliant detective novels.

—WJC

What people are saying about
NO PLACE TO HIDE:

NO PLACE TO HIDE is a tense, beautifully sculpted novel that blends international politics, the military, and of course crime. . . .When an author is able to strike a chord of fear with the opening lines, the reader can be assured the designated genre of 'suspense novel' is correct. Steve does this with direct ease. . . . . And [after this opening], we're off and running and that [fast, tense] pace is sustained throughout this fine book. . . .Reading this second installment of the Trace Austin series develops a need to read the entire series — and that is a solid sign that Steven M. Roth is a novelist of significance.

—Grady Harp, AMAZON HALL OF
FAME TOP 100 REVIEWER

What people are saying about
NO SAFE PLACE:

Steven Roth has written a terrifyingly real bioweapon suspense novel. He has the chops to keep a reader turning pages and anxious about what comes next. *No Safe Place* alerts us to what the government has done and may still be doing to an unsuspecting and unconcerned public. Highly recommended.

—Charlie Stella
Author of *TOMMY RED* and eight other crime novels

What people are saying about
MANDARIN YELLOW

A splendidly told and sophisticated tale by a first-time novelist. The multi-layered murder mystery not only remains engaging throughout, but also offers the reader a superb primer on Chinese culture and history, particularly post-World War II history.

If you're a mystery fan, you shouldn't miss this novel that features a Parker Duofold (the eponymous Mandarin Yellow). This is prime mystery: well plotted and compellingly written. Roth weaves a taut storyline, paces it perfectly, and wraps it in twists and turns that make no sense until you get to the end (when everything clicks perfectly into place). Along the way, he slips in all the clues you need to solve the mystery right along with hero Socrates Cheng.

STEVEN M. ROTH

DEATH OF THE YELLOW SWAN

DEATH
OF THE
YELLOW
SWAN

A 1930S SHANGHAI MURDER MYSTERY

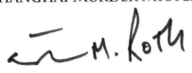

STEVEN M. ROTH

BLACKSTONE PRESS

A CRIME BOOK IMPRINT

MYSTERY AND SUSPENSE/THRILLER NOVELS BY STEVEN M. ROTH

Socrates Cheng Mystery Series:
MANDARIN YELLOW
THE MOURNING WOMAN
THE COUNTERFEIT TWIN

Trace Austin Suspense/Thriller Series:
NO SAFE PLACE
NO PLACE TO HIDE

1930s-Shanghai Mystery Series:
DEATH IN THE FLOWERY KINGDOM
DEATH OF THE YELLOW SWAN

Children's Mystery Book:
THE MYSTERY OF THE MISSING DONUT
A Mystery Introducing Owen Roth, Boy Detective

With Owen M. Roth
THE DOG WHO PLAYED CENTERFIELD
A Baseball Story

Published by Blackstone Press, a Crime Book Imprint

Cover design by Streetlight Graphics, LLC

ISBN: 978-1-7328748-3-1

FIRST EDITION

Visit the author's website: www.StevenMRoth.com

Contact the author at: http://www.stevenmroth.com/ContactMe.aspx

For Dominica and Owen

A NOTE ON SPELLING, ETC.

Throughout this novel, I have used the Wade-Giles romanizations of Chinese names, provinces, rivers, creeks, towns, cities, and Chinese expressions. This transliteration format was in common use in Shanghai in 1937.

AUTHOR'S WARNING TO READERS

This novel is not politically correct.

The story takes place in Shanghai in 1937. Many of the customs, statements, attitudes, and outlooks prevalent at that time not only might be alien to what we believe or accept in the twenty-first century, but also might be offensive to some people if portrayed in a novel set in the present-day.

Since **DEATH OF THE YELLOW SWAN** is a 1930s novel, I have tried to reflect the lives, language, and attitudes of the expatriates and Shanghainese people as they existed then, based on my research into then-contemporary English-language newspapers published in Shanghai, and also as reflected in personal journals published later. In doing so, I have not considered twenty-first century language, customs or sensibilities in writing this story. I use the slang and terminology used in 1937.

If this might bother you, I suggest that you not read this book.

PART ONE

CHAPTER 1

WAS IN MY OFFICE ON Bubbling Well Road in the International Settlement, putting the finishing touches on my report of a case I'd just investigated for a client, when someone pounded his fist on my door.

I recognized the insistent style of the strike. This was not a casual visitor or a potential client coming to see me. They would have just opened the door and walked in. This was the sound of some Shanghai Municipal Police (SMP) cop asserting his authority over me by demanding I walk over and open the door for him.

"*Qing! — Please!* Come in," I said, not getting up from my desk. "The door's not locked."

A uniformed SMP constable stepped into my office, slammed the door closed, and rapidly strode across the room toward me. His face was flushed.

I froze. *Was I about to be arrested?*

"Are you Ling Sun-jin?" he said, as he loomed over my desk.

I debated saying no to buy time to get away, to escape arrest and certain punishment for working without a private investigator's license and without a permit to carry a pistol, but decided this would be an exercise in futility. If the authorities knew about my unlawful PI business and had sent a patrolman to arrest me, any attempt to escape now would be pointless. And, even if I escaped, I would always be a fugitive in my home city.

As a fugitive, to survive, I would have to permanently leave Shanghai and take up residence somewhere else in China. But that was unthinkable. Except for the four years my elder brother and I attended college in the United States many years ago, I've spent my entire life in Shanghai. I would not even know where to go if I escaped. I would be an unemployed stranger in any other city.

"Who wants to know?" I asked, trying to sound unconcerned.

"I thought so. *Shi — Yes.* You match the description I was given."

"*Qivng rang? — Excuse me?* Given by who?" I said. I folded my hands together in front of me on my desk, trying to appear relaxed.

"I have a message for you." He looked hard into my eyes. "Chief Inspector Chapman wants you to come see him at headquarters within the half hour. He said to tell you this is not a request. He expects you there within thirty minutes."

Gaisi! — Damn! I thought. *Why does he want to see me? We haven't spoken since he fired me two years ago.*

I nodded at the constable, still hoping to appear unfazed by his message. But I wasn't unfazed. His message worried me since I've been secretly working as an unlicensed PI ever since the Municipal Council, acting on the chief inspector's recommendation, denied my application for a PI's license and for a permit to carry a pistol.

Has Chapman somehow found out I've been working in the shadows representing criminal-triad members when they needed my help?

The more I thought about this, the more I doubted it. I've been very careful to keep out of sight and to maintain a low profile when I've investigated cases.

Besides, Chief Inspector Chapman was a man who did things by the book. If he knew I was operating unlawfully, he wouldn't have sent only one uniformed foot-patrol constable to my office with a message summoning me. He would have sent a full squad of SMP constables to arrest me.

So, I wondered, *why, after all this time, did the chief inspector order me to his office to meet with him?*

I would soon find out.

CHAPTER 2

ONE DAY EARLIER

THERE WAS GENERAL AGREEMENT AMONG those who had seen her singing performances in Shanghai over the past three years: The Yellow Swan was a stunning and erotic young woman.

She was pencil thin, standing approximately 1.7 meters tall, and weighing 57kg. That, as the expatriate Americans in Shanghai would say, was approximately 5' 9" tall, and 126 pounds.

She had shiny, blue-black hair, the tips of which brushed her shoulders as she walked. Her coal-black eyes could burn a hole through a man or woman if she chose to do so, and she'd done just that on more than one occasion when sufficiently provoked by some member of her audience.

Her neck was slender and long like that of a swan, her skin slightly yellow, having the blended luster of someone born of parents whose ancestral stock originated in both the Celestial Middle Kingdom of China and in the Tokugawa Shogunate stock of Japan.

Only one resident in Shanghai, other than the young woman herself, knew her real name or where she had lived before 1934, when she arrived in the city. She seemed to have just appeared one day on Shanghai's theatrical scene. She'd been an instant entertainment sensation.

She was known in Shanghai by her entertaining name — the *Yellow Swan*.

When asked her true name or where she'd been raised by her parents, the Yellow Swan invariably laughed aside the question, without giving any other response. She intentionally, as she had been instructed to do, maintained an aura of mystery about herself.

The Yellow Swan worked in Shanghai as a chanteuse — a song stylist in a nightclub — at the Cathay Hotel, located at No. 20, the Bund. She was accompanied in her performances each night by Henry Washington's *All American Colored Dance Orchestra*, a jazz band imported from Kansas City in the United States. Together, Henry Washington and the Yellow Swan sought to satisfy Shanghai's unslakable thirst for American jazz and popular show tunes. They performed three shows each night during the week and four shows each night on weekends. Their performances were always sold out.

In the years she performed at the Cathay Hotel, the Yellow Swan missed only two shows. On those consecutive occasions, she'd been ill from the effects of having taken in too much opium earlier in the afternoon.

Tonight was different. The Yellow Swan was about to miss this night's performances for a far more serious reason than her addiction.

The Yellow Swan laid on the floor of her changing room, her neck broken, her larynx crushed.

The Yellow Swan had sung her last song.

CHAPTER 3

HIS NAME IS TU YUESHENG. Those who might speak about him did so only in hushed tones, and usually referred to him as Big-Eared Tu, although never to his face. Had anyone ever made that mistake, that person very likely would have died a certain and very slow, painful death.

Big-Eared Tu was a man always to be reckoned with. His genius was that he had vision, supreme cunning, absolute ruthlessness, and a successful gambler's sixth sense. Other than Generalissimo Chiang Kai-shek, who headed China's Nationalist Kuomintang army (referred to as the KMT), Tu was the most powerful man in China, in all of its major cities — in Shanghai and Peking, in Tientsin, and in Canton, among others. In Shanghai, especially, the site of his home and headquarters, Tu, when it came to acquiring and maintaining power, took a backseat to no one. Not even to General Chiang Kai-shek.

The 1936 edition of *Who's Who in Shanghai* described Tu as a well-known and respected public-welfare worker, who was a prominent member of the French Concession's Municipal Council, the president of two privately-owned banks, a director sitting on the boards of several private businesses, and the chairman of the Constancy Society — an organization created by Tu to unite behind him the many protégés and triad-gang members he'd gathered about him over the years.

All in all, if the portrait drawn of him by *Who's Who* was to be believed, Big-Eared Tu was, on paper at least, a benevolent old man who spoke softly — especially when he was angry — who dressed in the long-silk gowns of a Mandarin scholar, and who routinely performed good deeds and other acts of charity.

But, in reality, Big-Eared Tu was anything but benevolent. He had cruelty in his dead eyes and a knife's edge in his soft voice. He was not a man to trifle with.

CHAPTER 4

NOW THAT I AM NO longer an inspector detective with the Special Branch of the SMP, people call me by my first name, Sun-jin, rather than address me as Inspector Detective, as they did before.

I am thirty-seven years old, Chinese on my father's side and British on my mother's side. To all appearances, I look full-blooded Chinese, with my yellow-tinted skin and with epicanthic folds over my eyes, making them appear narrow and slanted.

Because of my blended blood, neither the British expatriates in Shanghai nor the Chinese natives accept me as their own. I am considered to be a mongrel, a *low faan* — a *half-breed* — and, therefore, considered inferior by both cultures.

Ever since Chief Inspector Chapman fired me two years ago for insubordination, and then blocked my ability to obtain a PI's license and a weapon permit, I have worked in the shadows as an unlicensed private investigator, serving low-level triad members and special, illicit business interests. That also means I carry a pistol without having the permit the municipal council requires. To do otherwise in this dangerous city and in this business would be suicidal.

The penalty for both these infractions, if I'm caught, would be severe. Up until now, I didn't think I had to worry because I've been prudent in my PI activities, keeping a low profile, never openly stirring the pot. *But,* I thought, *perhaps I miscalculated somewhere along the line. Otherwise, why would the chief inspector have summoned me to his office this morning?*

I walked into the SMP headquarters, located on Pingliang Road in the International Settlement, and told the desk-sergeant I was there to see Chief Inspector Chapman, that he was expecting me.

"Sit," Sun-jin," Chapman said. "You look good, Old Boy, all things considered."

I nodded and took the seat he offered me in front of his desk. I was nervous. My right knee would not stop bouncing as I sat. I furtively held it down with my hand to hide its activity.

"I'm well, sir. And you?"

He stood up from behind his desk, walked over to the office door, and closed it. He returned to his seat.

"Just to clear the air and to set matters in their proper perspective before we get to why I asked you here, I should tell you I know you've been working unlawfully as a PI, and that you own several guns, although you were denied a license to work and a permit to have any guns."

"Sir, I can ex—"

Chapman raised his palm and stopped me.

"That's not why you're here, Sun-jin. If that was the issue for me, I would have had you arrested months ago. I've closed my eyes to your indiscretion because of your years of loyal service to the SMP, and because you've kept a low profile as a PI, not flaunting your disregard for our licensing and permit laws."

I was confused, but grateful to the chief inspector.

"Thank you, sir."

"You're here, Old Boy, because we — I mean *you* — have a serious problem in the Settlement. I want you to resolve it for us, for me and you," he said.

That surprised me. "Yes, sir, of course. How can I—"

The chief inspector looked away from me, stopping me in mid-sentence. He pulled out his pipe, slowly packed its bowl with tobacco, tamped the tobacco down with the brown-stained end of his thumb, then applied a lighted match to the top of the bowl. He drew heavily on the pipe until it burned on its own. He blew out the match and looked up at me when he finished.

"It goes without saying that what I'm about to tell you must remain confidential. No one is to know about it, not even anyone from the SMP. Only me."

I nodded. "Yes, sir. I understand."

"All right, then," he said. "Here's the problem. . . ."

CHAPTER 5

K ANJI GORŌ, A TWENTY-NINE YEAR old Yakuza member, a skilled swordsman, martial artist, and *Bo Shuriken* throwing-star master, born of Japanese parents, but now living in Peking, was one of Yakuza's most skilled assassins. He'd been a member of Yakuza — the *Extreme Path Society* crime syndicate located in Japan and abroad — since 1916, from three days after his eleventh birthday.

Like many Yakuza members, Kanji had occasionally violated its strict code of conduct, but never so severely as to have been required to forfeit his own life, as some other Yakuza members he'd known had been required to do. Kanji's infractions had been such as to be considered minor, but punishable nevertheless, so that what he suffered for his transgressions was the same punishment as other members who had committed minor offenses — a fated ritual known in Japan as *Yubitsume* — the severing of part of the pinky finger as an act of penance and apology. Kanji, for his first code infraction was required to chop off the first digit of the little finger of his left hand. Since that time, Kanji had been required to sever the outer digits of two other fingers.

Kanji approached the leader of his Peking Yakuza cell, the group's surrogate father — known as the *Oyabun* — with all the deference and trepidation of a recalcitrant, surrogate child — a *Kobun*.

Kanji bowed, waited until his presence was acknowledged with a nod, then lowered himself before the *Oyabun*, prostrating himself before his leader, his forehead touching the floor.

"Honorable, *Oyabun*," Kanji said. "May I speak?"

His surrogate father nodded again and said, "Speak, my son."

His forehead still touching the floor, Kanji said, "I seek your permission to go to Shanghai to fulfill a personal mission."

"Describe your desire."

"The woman I've loved for twelve years — Matsuko Akasuki — has been murdered in Shanghai. I wish to go to that city, locate her killer, avenge her death, and restore her honor, as well as the honor of her family and ancestors. Then I will return to our family."

The clan leader looked down at Kanji. "Stand," he said.

Kanji stood and faced his surrogate father.

"You have my permission to go on your mission. But you understand our code. Merely by undertaking this, means that your mission is not personal. It is a mission of our family. Should you fail, your penalty will not be *Yubitsume*. It will require *Seppuku, Hara Kiri* — *your ritual death by your own hand.*"

"I understand, *Oyabun*."

Before you depart, then, we will formalize, by our ceremonial sharing of a cup of Saki, our bond as a *Tekiya* — *a family*. Then you will have my blessing to seek your vengeance.

A cup of Saki was immediately produced by a servant who'd been standing nearby.

Kanji sipped from the ceremonial cup, then handed it to the *Oyabun*.

The elderly man took a sip of the rice wine, then said, "Go, *my Kobun — my son*. Return to your family when you have accomplished our family's mission.

Three days later, Kanji left Peking and traveled to Shanghai, bringing with him the lethal tools of his trade.

CHAPTER 6

T WENTY-EIGHT YEAR OLD WU MEI-HUA impatiently tapped her foot on the dirt sidewalk, just outside the entrance to Sincere department store, while she waited for Chiang Kai-shek's three KMT soldiers to inspect her identity papers. She was used to this procedure. This had been going on in Shanghai since 1927, when Chiang launched his abhorrent Bandit Extermination Campaign against members of the Chinese Communist Party (CCP), against trade union members, and against leftist high school and university students who frequently protested against Chiang's rule of China. Mei-hua's familiarity with the ritual did not ameliorate her hatred of it nor of the man who had instituted the process.

Mei-hua, toned and muscular from her daily *Shaolin* martial arts practice, had no doubt that in hand-to-hand combat she could easily defeat these three soldiers, but then what would she do? *Become a fugitive from my home city?* she thought. *No, she would be patient for now and would put up with these fools.*

———❖———

The young soldier glanced at her papers, compared Mei-hua's photo-ID to the flesh and blood young woman standing before him, then nodded and smiled at her as he extended his hand holding her papers toward her.

"*Xiexie — All right.* Everything seems in order," he said. "Move along then, young woman, unless you would prefer to exercise the special privilege I'm about to offer you to join us for a glass of beer when we finish our rounds in twenty minutes." He looked over and grinned at his companions as he offered his invitation to Mei-hua.

"In that case, walk with us until we are off-duty, when it will be our pleasure to drink with you, and then afterward for the three of us to pleasure you."

Mei-hua silently retrieved her papers from the soldier's grasp, refolded them, and placed them back in her shirt pocket. She said nothing in response to the soldier's invitation, but turned away from the three men and left. When she was a safe distance away, she turned slightly and furtively looked back at the soldiers.

Hun dan! — Assholes! she thought.

Mei-hua, an attractive young woman, wore her coal-black hair bobbed in the style of the young revolutionary she'd become. She typically wore long, loose-fitting pants and a peasant-style, coarsely-woven shirt.

She was the not-so-subtle product of her prescient, ambitious middle-class mother (herself the product of a successful Shanghai mercantile family), rather than a reflection of her career-minded military father whose abiding mission in life was to do whatever seemed necessary to advance his rank in Chiang's KMT army from that of colonel to the rank of general, as he fought the armed forces of the CCP.

In most ways, Mei-hua's mother, who'd had bound feet as a young girl, was old fashioned. She was orthodox in running her daily household, orthodox in her religious practices, and orthodox, too, in her general outlook concerning married life, nodding her head in agreement, for example, whenever Mei-hua's father spoke.

And yet one aspect of her life, in particular, bothered her. As she watched Mei-hua's three older brothers grow up, go off to private schools, and then return home full of new, unconventional ideas — ideas which they debated endlessly among themselves and with their father at the family's dinner table — she wondered why those modern ideas should not also apply to her only daughter, as well as to her three sons. Mei-hua's father was not able to answer that question when frequently asked to do so by his wife.

When Mei-hua became seven years old, her mother turned her attention to the then singular cause in her life — assuring that her daughter would receive an education.

Mei-hua's father resisted, but his wife was unrelenting in her quest. She employed all the weapons available to a woman in her position: tears, anger, pious entreaties, intrigue, cunning, and sex. She eventually won her point. Mei-hua's father agreed that their daughter could be educated, provided her tutor was an old-fashioned, elderly Confucian scholar who would come to their home to instruct Mei-hua only with respect to Mandarin characters, the practice of calligraphy, watercolor painting, and the writing of poetry. Nothing else.

During her eighth year with her tutor, days after her fifteenth birthday, rumors began to circulate in the Old City where the Wu family lived that Me-hua was not as obedient, in general, as girls were expected to be, even young girls raised by eccentric mothers and absentee fathers. Indeed, the wagging tongues said, Mei-hua, for many years, had been encouraged by her mother to be rebellious.

This came to a head when it became known that Mei-hua, although not a student at the local high school, had organized and successfully led a student strike against the corrupt administration of the school. She was sixteen years old at the time. When asked by her father why she had organized such a traitorous activity, Mei-hua responded that she had been inspired by the striking sales clerks at the Wing On department store, clerks who recently and notoriously had successfully gone on strike demanding that their working hours be reduced to twelve hours per day and that they only be required to work six days each week.

Mei-hua's mother, who gradually acquired complete control of the family while her soldier-husband was away for long periods fighting for the KMT against the CCP's army, instead of discouraging Mei-hua's radical activities, encouraged her daughter in her left-leaning endeavors.

When Mei-hua became seventeen, her mother fired Mei-hua's elderly, original Confucian tutor, and enrolled Mei-hua as a senior student in a modern school where she soon became the leader of several movements against Chiang's government and against the western powers occupying parts of Shanghai.

It was during this year in Mei-hua's formal education that she achieved her most notorious accomplishment. She convinced the school authorities, who wanted to avoid a student strike, to allow male and female students to study together. Even her mother disapproved of this, but she remained silent in the face of her daughter's enthusiasm and extraordinary achievement.

When, to the general relief of the school authorities, Mei-hua graduated from this high school, having been a student there for only one year, she enrolled in Shanghai University, a teachers' college which a recent student revolt had turned into a training ground for radical students. Mei-hua graduated from the university in two and one-half years with a degree in philosophy.

Now, finished with her basic university education, Mei-hua had a burning desire to remake China, to rid it of its many decadent practices such as the use of debilitating opium, the acceptance of concubinage, the pervasive influence of the western powers operating in Shanghai and elsewhere, and to rid it of those accepted Confucian and Taoist dogmas which venerated ones age over skills and merit.

Soon after graduating from Shanghai University, like many of the privileged children of wealthy middle-class parents, Mei-hua sought a foreign education to broaden her life experience. With her mother's blessing and her father's acquiescence, Mei-hua enrolled in Tokyo University, graduating with an advanced degree in political theory. Afterward, however, she refused to obey her father's order to return home to Shanghai. Instead, with her mother's approval, Mei-hua traveled to Russia and enrolled in Moscow University to study economics. She specialized in the theories of Karl Marx and Friedrich Engels.

Mei-hua returned to Shanghai, her degree from Moscow University in hand, shortly after her twenty-fifth birthday.

Two weeks later, restless in Shanghai, and with nothing for her to do there to aid the CCP, Mei-hua traveled to Canton, the mecca of the CCP's emerging revolution, and became a member of the Communist Party Youth Group. With that step, Mei-hua officially joined the Revolution, as the CCP's movement was called throughout China. Then she returned to Shanghai to advance its cause.

Two days after her twenty-sixth birthday, Mei-hua decided to escape the KMT's frequent and broadly targeted political murders, mass assassinations, and beheadings of CCP members and trade unionists in the streets of Shanghai. She had tired of seeing severed human heads jammed onto the tops of posts throughout the city, each with one ear missing to remind passersby that these all were political killings. Mei-hua left Shanghai and moved to the countryside where she became a member of the Revolutionary Tribunal that tried the enemies of the Revolution, confiscated the lands of rich landlords, and distributed those lands among the local peasants.

In October 1934, Mei-hua joined approximately 100,000 CCP soldiers of the First Central Red Army and 8,000 civilians who, to escape annihilation by Chiang's KMT army, walked to the mountains and caves of Xian in what would become known throughout China as the Long March.

Like most of her fellow marchers, however, Mei-hua soon was forced by illness — brought on by fatigue, cold, and hunger — to drop out of the Long March. After living with a peasant family for five months to regain her health and strength, Mei-hua returned to her parent's home in Shanghai to further recover. She later learned from newspaper reports that only 3,000 soldiers and a few hundred civilians had successfully completed the Long March. She also learned that the CCP's membership roster had dropped from 300,000 active members at the start of the Long March to about 40,000 members during the one-year journey. Things looked bleak for the CCP.

Mei-hua was disillusioned enough from her own experience on the Long March not to be surprised. At her mother's urging, Mei-hua followed the current trend in Shanghai and dropped her CCP membership.

In 1937, no longer an active part of the Revolution, Mei-hua seemed to have lost interest in the CCP. She retired altogether from activities related to that life, and stayed home in her parents' house, studying philosophy. Eventually, at her father's urging, she joined the KMT — the enemy of the CCP — as a civilian worker.

That was when Mei-hua decided she would become a spy to aid the Revolution.

CHAPTER 7

I RELAXED IN MY CHAIR AND waited to hear the confidential story Chief Inspector Chapman intended to tell me — the story he described as my problem, too, not only his. For some reason I did not know, my knee had finally stopped bouncing. This, of course, made no sense to me. I should have been — and was — very nervous about what the chief inspector might say and how it could affect my life. My knee should have been out of control.

"Do you agree to my terms concerning confidentiality?" Chapman said.

"*Shi — Yes.* Agreed, sir. Of course."

"Okay, then." He stared briefly at the closed office door as if trying to see through it and catch anyone who might be listening at the keyhole.

"A young woman was murdered the other evening at the Cathay Hotel. That's the luxury hotel owned by Victor Sassoon, in case you didn't know."

"I know that, sir."

The mention of Sassoon's name caught my attention and gave me pause. My knee jerked once. Sassoon was not a man to be trifled with. He was one of Shanghai's wealthiest players. He also had ruined my career as a SMP Special Branch inspector detective, causing me to be fired by the chief inspector.

"She worked at the Tower Club as a singer," the chief inspector said. "She was found dead last night in her changing room. Someone had snapped her neck.

"Even though less than twenty-four hours have passed," he added, "the press has begun to bay for blood. She was very popular with her fans."

I was curious to find out why the chief inspector thought it was necessary to have me involved in a routine murder investigation. This seemed to be an unremarkable homicide, if an unpopular one, but not one that called for the SMP's Special Branch to investigate. I remained quiet to hear what the chief inspector might say about that.

"We don't yet know the young woman's actual name, or, for that matter, anything about her before she came to Shanghai. She was known here in the entertainment industry as the Yellow Swan."

He paused briefly, then asked, "Ever hear of her?"

I shook my head. "No, sir. The Tower Club's too rich for my budget." I paused, then said, "*Ayeeyah!*" cursing in Mandarin, but then switching to English, "I have to ask, sir, are you sure this was a homicide, not just an accident, a fall?"

"We're sure."

"Then I have another question, if I may. What's so special about her death that you want me involved? It sounds like a routine SMP matter, not even a Special Branch matter."

The chief inspector ignored my question.

"The young woman had a Chinese mother, but a Jap father," the chief inspector said. "In Shanghai's current political climate, with the Jap army waiting for an excuse to pounce on us, that's a combustible mix, as you know."

I did know.

Even though the two cultures historically had gotten along, with Japan often acting as the mentor, and China acting as the mentored civilization, the two cultures recently had become enemies, so that such a marriage between citizens of the two currently antagonistic cultures, even though accepted when the marriage had originally occurred, now was frowned upon by both countries.

But I didn't see why this should cause the Municipal Council or the chief inspector any special problem. After all, a homicide was a homicide, and all homicides were investigated according to established procedures. The culture or ethnicity of the victim or of the victim's parents should have been irrelevant, especially in this roiling Asian cauldron we call Shanghai, with its traditional stew of competing populations, rival militaries, disparate cultures, and conflicting political interests.

But I was wrong.

The chief inspector continued. "The Municipal Council is concerned that the Japs will use the young woman's death as an excuse to declare a political incident, as they did in 1932.

"The Council wants to avoid a controversy that might be used by the Japs to take short-term military action against the city — especially, in this case, since such military action might necessarily involve the British and Americans because the murder took place in the Settlement.

"The Japs," he said, "already are insisting that they take control of the investigation, although, as you know, the Japanese Municipal Police (JMP) jurisdiction does not extend outside Hongkew."

"*Dui bu qi — Sorry,*" I said, then switched from Mandarin back to English, having remembered who I was speaking to.

"I understand, sir, but I still don't see why or how you think I can help you with this. Why not just use an SMP inspector detective to investigate the crime? Why call on me?"

Again the chief inspector ignored my question.

"I want you to investigate the young woman's murder, and solve it before the political situation gets out of hand. I don't want the Japs to use this as an excuse to provoke an incident or to bomb the Settlement, as they bombed the Old City in '32."

This still puzzled me. He still hadn't answered my question. I tried again. "But why me, Chief Inspector? Any experienced Special Branch inspector detective can do the same thing you're asking me to do."

"Expediency is why, Old Boy. You can avoid the red tape and inevitable delays an SMP inspector detective must deal with. You can move the inquiry along, avoiding the rules and protocols that slow down a normal homicide investigation.

"Speed is important in the current political climate," he said. "We need to wrap this up quickly before the Japs use it as an excuse to take military action."

He glanced down at his pipe, put another match to its bowl, drew the smoke into his mouth, and then let it out.

"I want this investigated on two tracks, each to be independent from the other. Your investigation will be kept secret from the official SMP investigator, who will follow the required protocols and will become ensnared in reports and other red tape."

"Meaning what, sir?"

"Meaning, I will have the Special Branch investigate the murder at the same time you also investigate it. The SMP's investigation will be for the Council's, the Jap's, and the public's consumption and benefit. Your investigation will be for my benefit, and will be intended to head off an international incident. You will conduct it in secret."

I must have frowned because as I opened my mouth to ask what, specifically, that meant, the chief inspector held up his palm again to stop me from speaking.

"Hear me out, Sun-jin, then ask your questions."

As always, the chief inspector showed himself to be a courteous man, although he seemed to me this time to be disturbed by the situation he had described.

"Yes, sir." I leaned back in my chair to listen to what he had to say.

"The SMP will conduct a normal homicide investigation, going through all the usual steps necessary to assure the Japs we are taking this matter seriously. Hopefully, that will appease them, although I'm not optimistic it will.

"Whoever officially investigates this crime for the SMP will have to be sensitive to its political aspects. That could well limit or undermine the SMP's investigation. But doing it that way will be necessary."

I nodded. I understood that much from my years in the Special Branch.

"That's one aspect of this, Sun-jin. Then, while the official SMP investigation goes forward, I want you to conduct your own murder investigation, untainted by politics and red tape, and, as I said, conduct it in secret.

"You will not have the resources of our crime lab to fall back on, and will not be able to see our investigative files. Doing so might expose what you're doing.

"You will have to avoid being discovered by the SMP

inspector detective who is investigating the crime, of course, as you uncover and investigate the same witnesses and the same evidence he is. You will have to function, in the words of Lao Tzu, as a 'good runner, leaving no footprints.'

"That, I think, might be your biggest challenge. But it will be absolutely necessary that you not be uncovered by the SMP as part of the official investigation or by the Japs as they try to provoke a military incident."

The chief inspector was concerned about protecting his back. *What about my back?* I wondered.

I decided I had to say something before this went too far and my involvement became inevitable. I didn't think the chief inspector's expectations of the situation and what I could do under the conditions he'd just imposed on me were realistic or achievable.

Beyond that, I had no interest in being involved in this sure-to-fail situation. It seemed to me that I could only come out of this with greater enmity from the Municipal Council, the chief inspector, and from the SMP Special Branch, than I already shouldered. This was a setup sure to fail and to cause me problems later on.

"*Qing — Please.* If I might say so, sir, this sounds like a potential nightmare, an assignment bound to fail before it even gets started."

Chapman looked down at the bowl of his pipe and frowned. This, clearly, was not what he wanted to hear. When he looked up at me again, his face was pinched and flushed.

I said, "Being found out by the SMP detective is likely unavoidable if he does his job right since we'll have to cross paths as we pursue the same evidence and witnesses.

"As for keeping the investigation secret from the Dwarf

Bandits — the Japanese — well, I just don't know if it's possible, no matter how many precautions I might take."

The chief inspector looked hard at me and slowly shook his head.

"It will be your responsibility, Sun-jin, to avoid being discovered. If you fail, I'll deny we ever had this conversation. I'll also prosecute you for having engaged in unlawful PI activity and for carrying a pistol without a permit."

Fankwei! — *foreign devil!* I thought. *Typical Round-Eyes threat. If you don't get your way with the local Chinese, threaten or punish them.*

"May I think about this, Chief Inspector?" I asked. "I can give you my answer tomorrow morning."

I needed time to come to grips with what the chief inspector wanted, and I wanted to understand the consequences of everything involved before I agreed to take this on. There was too much at stake for me to just reflexively agree.

"No. I want your answer right now. If you decline to take this on, then we will talk about your unlawful activities, and will proceed to deal with those crimes."

Damn Englishman, I thought. I did not expect this treatment, not even from this high-handed British bureaucrat who used to be my boss and sometimes pretended to be my friend.

I stared out the window briefly, as if in deep thought. I already knew my answer.

"Well, Sun-jin, what's it to be?"

The chief inspector impatiently tapped his pipe against the edge of a thick, dark-amber glass ashtray sitting on his desk, dislodging foul-smelling black ashes from the pipe's bowl.

I forced my facial expression and my tone of voice to seem

neutral. "I'll do it, sir, of course, but I would like you to do something for me in return."

The chief inspector frowned. "What's that, Old Boy?"

"Have the Council reverse its previous decisions and grant me a PI license and pistol permit. I'd like the approvals to be retroactive to the dates of my applications two years ago."

"That's not going to happen," the chief inspector said, not even taking time to pretend to think about my request. "I'm not even willing to try. You made too many enemies in high places for that to succeed.

"Besides, it would raise questions from the Council why I now want to aid you this way after I recommended before that they deny your applications." He slowly shook his head as he said this.

I wasn't surprised by his answer.

"I see, sir. Well, then, I guess I'll get started on the homicide."

"Not quite yet, Sun-jin. You need to be aware of some other essential conditions for you to follow." He again paused to tap his pipe against the ashtray.

"You are to confine your investigation to the Settlement. There are to be no searches, inquiries or other activities in the French Concession or elsewhere."

"Sir? That's not a good idea. I should follow the evidence where it takes me."

The chief inspector shook his head. "No. Not this time. You're likely to provoke an incident if you take your inquiry too much afar. I have to be firm on this," he said.

I remained silent. What could I say.

"Another thing," he said, as if I hadn't just agreed to his impossible conditions in connection with performing a task that couldn't possibly succeed. "You will report only to me. And only in person. Not on the telephone.

"Set up a way to let me know when and where you want to meet. Make it someplace no one who knows us might see us together or might find out about our meeting."

"Yes, sir."

He glared at me for a moment as if trying to decide if he wanted to say something else.

"There's one more thing. This is crucial. You have only one week, or maybe even less, to solve the murder. Any more time, and this will likely evolve into an official incident with the Japs.

"We can hold them off for maybe one week, I think, but not for more than that before they react badly." He looked away from me as he finished saying this.

"One week?" I blurted out. I couldn't believe he was restricting me this way. "But almost no homicide can be solved in—"

"One week or maybe less, that's all," he said. "After that, it will be as if you refused to take on this case. In that event, I'll be forced to proceed to prosecute you. That's how important this is."

"Yes, sir," I said. I took a deep breath. My knee bounced again. I made no effort to control it. I bit my lower lip until it hurt.

The chief inspector and I discussed the best way for me to approach my investigation, given the restrictions he had just placed on me. He had no suggestions for me, but he did give me some information to get me started.

He told me that the autopsy and the preliminary investigation overnight by the SMP had produced no important information or clues other than the conclusion that the Yellow

Swan's death had not been an accident. In fact, he said, the SMP had no clues at all, although they preliminarily have ruled out robbery as a motive since the Yellow Swan, when found, still was wearing her jewelry.

The chief inspector walked me to his office door.

"Don't let me down, Sun-jin."

CHAPTER 8

DAY ONE OF THE INVESTIGATION

I LEFT THE CHIEF INSPECTOR'S OFFICE and headed home to my apartment in the northern walled section of the International Settlement, that part of Shanghai known as Chapei. To those of us who were raised here, it more commonly is referred to as the Old City. I have lived in Chapei, by choice, all my life, even though for many years I was able to afford to move to a better apartment building and to settle in a more modern neighborhood.

Chapei is noisy, dirty, and bursting with people who are crowded into buildings not sufficiently large enough to comfortably hold them and their families or their businesses.

I know my love for the Old City is anomalous, especially since I even love the grinding, grating, clanging, and banging racket of Chapei — the around-the-clock commotion in the streets, the constant cacophony we Chinese take for granted and refer to as *jenao*.

I love it all: the sounds of electric trolleys with their screeching wheels and clanging bells; the rickshaw coolies yelling to attract fares or screaming at one another to get out of the way; the street hawkers announcing their goods for sale; the barbers who clang their *huan tou* — tuning forks — to call customers out from buildings to come down to the street to receive a haircut; the car horns honking; the people doing business deals in the middle of the street without regard to the danger from swarming vehicles; and, the pedestrians clogging the sidewalks, talking to others in raised voices so as to be heard above the general ruckus. I love it all.

I have lived with *jenao* all my life — except for the years I was in the United States at the university — and never feel comfortable or in place when I am in some other part of Shanghai, such as some neighborhoods in the French Concession that are quiet and orderly. This is my Shanghai — Chapei, the Old City — the place where I was born and have always lived, so that, at any intersection or on any street, I need merely turn my head to see landmarks or buildings that stir-up memories for me.

For all that, however, I have chosen to live in great comfort within Chapei. My apartment building was one of the first modern structures built on Golden Karp Avenue. Although the rent in this building ordinarily would have been beyond my means, even when I was working as an SMP Special Branch inspector detective, and was bringing home a decent salary, I am able to rent my apartment cheaply. That's because my apartment is located on the building's fourth floor and, therefore, was difficult for the landlord to rent to anyone else. Why? Because we Chinese detest the number four. To us, it sounds like the Mandarin word for death. The fourth floors of apartment and office buildings, therefore, are often difficult to rent, so I leased my apartment at a bargain price.

Physically, however, the rest of my street still is typical of the Old City with regard to its buildings: one-story shacks; street markets; open-front shops during the day that are closed-up at night or in troubled times by the lowering of steel shutters; pawn shops, medicine shops, ramshackle restaurants or food stalls; and, open-air butchers and screeching vegetable hawkers, among other merchants.

Golden Karp Avenue has it all. There are vendors standing at street corners with baskets of fruit dangling from bamboo poles balanced on their shoulders; there are bathhouses, fortune-tellers, professional letter writers — scholars who'd failed their civil service examinations, and who, for payment, write letters for illiterate people — money changers, singers who entertain passers-by for payment, and, acrobats and street magicians performing for donations.

The first thing I did upon arriving home was refresh the water bowl for my pet dog, *Bik — Jade*. When she finished drinking, and I had petted her until she seemed restless with my doting, I walked her downstairs and turned her loose outside for the rest of the day.

I poured myself a tall glass of *Shaojiu* rice wine, took a pencil and paper from my desk drawer, and sat down to plan a strategy for investigating my new case. I started by naming the case: The Death of the Yellow Swan.

I decided I would begin my investigation by following established, proven investigatory procedures. I would try to reconstruct the Yellow Swan's last days before she died. I would start with the last known sightings of the young woman, and work back in time, carefully, but swiftly because murder investigations must move fast or they quickly grind to a halt as evidence trails run cold, witnesses disappear or forget what they saw or know, or they reimagine what they have seen or heard. That all allows killers to escape.

I would interview the Yellow Swan's colleagues at the Tower Club, and talk to neighborhood shopkeepers, rickshaw pullers, taxi drivers, and staff at the Cathay Hotel, all to see if anyone could tell me about the Yellow Swan's last days. The murder was still recent enough that memories should still be fresh.

Having decided on this general course of action, I next listed the obstacles I would face under the chief inspector's restrictive rules:

No more than seven days to identify the murderer, maybe fewer if the Dwarf Bandits threatened to provoke an incident

I must proceed in secret

I would have no access to the usual SMP reports or to the lab work from the crime scene

I would lack the implicit authority, as a Special Branch inspector detective has, to coerce witnesses into cooperating

That all seemed to present me with a pretty grim picture of what would hinder me during my investigation.

I next listed the positive aspects of my investigation:

No SMP rules and regulations to restrict me

No reports and other paperwork to prepare and submit

I would not be jailed for having worked as an unlicensed PI

I would not be jailed for having carried an unlicensed pistol

On balance, I decided, the negative aspects of the investigation outweighed the positive ones, other than the fact that I would not be arrested if I solved the murder in a timely fashion.

Since the Yellow Swan had been a celebrity in Shanghai these past three years, I assumed her death would be reported the local newspapers.

I looked for and found a copy of this morning's *North-China Daily News*. Then I looked in the paper for the story of the Yellow Swan's murder. The newspaper ran the small headline: The YELLOW Swan IS DEAD.

The article did not give me any information about the Yellow Swan herself I hadn't already learned from Chief Inspector Chapman. It offered me nothing new about my victim. But one piece of information reported in the newspaper was new: Inspector Detective Ma Wang of the SMP Special Branch, a former colleague of mine, was named in the newspaper as the person in charge of the official investigation. Now I knew who I had to avoid.

To give the article color, the reporter made much of the fact that no one knew anything about the Yellow Swan's background. To fill in the lean article, the reporter relied on rumor and gossip offered by people who had worked with the Yellow Swan at the Tower Club. I made a few notes from the article.

According to the reporter, the Yellow Swan had begun singing at the Cathay Hotel's Tower Club in August 1934, and regularly performed there until her death. The article indicated that her co-workers stated that she'd been well-liked by them, although she did not seem to have any friends among the other entertainers or other employees at the club. No one knew her real name. No one could say why she kept her actual name a secret, and why she insisted that she be called or referred to as the Yellow Swan.

Furthermore, according to the story, no one was able to give a reason or a motive for her murder. Nor could I, based on what I'd read in the newspaper or based on what the chief inspector had told me. But one thing seemed clear to me from the article: This was not a killing by an amateur, nor was it a failed robbery. As the chief inspector had indicated, the Yellow Swan neck had been thoroughly, cleanly snapped, and she still was wearing her jewelry when she was found.

The reporter had asked, and had written in his article: Did anyone ever ask the Yellow Swan why she was so secretive?

"Several of us did," one woman answered.

"And?" the reporter followed up.

"And the Yellow Swan merely smiled, shrugged, and wouldn't tell," the woman said.

CHAPTER 9

DAY ONE OF THE INVESTIGATION

The first thing I did after I finished reading the *North-China Daily News* article was to go to the public library to begin the arduous task of paging through back copies of Shanghai newspapers — the *North-China Daily News*, the *Shanghai Times*, the *North China Star*, and other local papers. I knew this would take a few hours, at best, and likely not produce any useful information about the Yellow Swan's background, but this was a basic step I could not pass by. I would limit this research for now to local newspapers published over the past three years, beginning in August 1934, when the Yellow Swan started working at the Tower Club. Later, perhaps tomorrow, I would expand my search to cover out-of-town newspapers.

After four hours with no results, I left the library.

I moved onward in my investigation. I turned back to the lists I'd made, now adding information on how I would approach my investigation within the framework (or, is it, within the confines) of my very short, allowable period-of-time to solve the crime.

I started a third list, setting out steps I planned to take to investigate the case. My entries into the third list seemed pretty obvious to me: I would use known informants to learn information about the Yellow Swan, tapping into the vast group of triad members I had developed as paid sources these past two years. I wrote down the names of informants I thought would be useful to my investigation.

I also would create a Murder Book, as I'd always done when I was with the SMP, because the homicide inspector detective's 3-ring-binder Murder Book is his case bible as the investigation proceeds. It is a key investigatory tool, for it allows the investigator not only to see individual pieces of evidence, but also see patterns among the evidence.

An official SMP Murder Book contains everything about a homicide that the investigating inspector detectives can put together, both official and unofficial, and so would mine, to the extent possible. The goal would be to have everything pertinent to the case available in one place.

The official Murder Book incorporates information about every suspect, every person of interest, every person interviewed by the inspector detectives, every piece of physical evidence, all crime scene photographs, all the field and lab reports, and the information concerning every witness and the victim, including transcripts of interviews, autopsy reports, and all results from that new science they call forensics. My murder book would be far more limited because it would not contain official SMP lab and other reports.

Finally, I would see if I could tie the Yellow Swan's death to any other recent murders in Shanghai involving performers in the entertainment industry. I also would see if I could link the Yellow Swan's death to any other mysterious deaths that had occurred in the International Settlement, in the French Concession, or in the Hongkew section of the Settlement. I would do this even though the chief inspector told me to limit my investigation to the International Settlement. I couldn't be so geographically constrained if the evidence led me elsewhere. Not if I hoped to solve the crime within seven days.

I set the three lists aside and thought about what I knew so far about the case and what I reasonably could assume based on the little I knew. I also considered what more I wanted to know.

After thirty minutes, I changed out of my day-to-day work clothes and put on my best wool suit, a clean linen shirt, and a pre-knotted necktie. I pomaded my hair with Brilliantine, combed it straight back from my forehead, and left my apartment to visit the crime scene.

CHAPTER 10

DAY ONE OF THE INVESTIGATION

As I left my apartment building to walk to the electric trolley so I could ride it over to the Cathay Hotel, I saw Bik across the street looking at me and wagging her tail. I called her over, knelt down, then patted her head and stroked her back. For some reason, doing this to her reminded me of a great debt I owed my dog, for thanks to Bik, approximately fourteen months ago I met the woman I have come to love.

This occurred when I had been headed to Nanking Road, the International Settlement's principle retail shopping street, on which are located, among other shops, the Chocolate Shop (a popular rendezvous for Americans), Sun Ya (a popular Chinese restaurant patronized by westerners), Lao Kai Fook and Lao Kai Chuang (Shanghai's two leading silk shops), and several of the large, modern department stores (such as Sincere and Double Sun shopping emporiums) found in Shanghai.

I'd had shopping to do that day at the Wing On department store. I took Bik with me that morning.

Because dogs are not allowed in Wing On, yet we Chinese have always insisted on bringing our pets everywhere we go, the store provides a grassy, fenced-in compound where shoppers can leave their dogs while they are in the store. I tied Bik to a post, using a long leash so she could wander within the outdoor pen, and left her there while I shopped.

When I finished, as I approached the dog compound, I saw a young woman squatting back on her heels next to Bik, petting Bik's head and back. I walked up to them.

Bik abruptly stood up, looked at me, and furiously wagged her tail as I came close.

The young woman looked up at me, too. She seemed tense as I approached. She slowly stood up.

"*Heya — Hello.* Is this your dog?" she said, speaking Mandarin.

"*Shi — Yes.* Her name is Bik."

"She needs water. It's too hot for her to be tied up out here, even in the morning shade."

Ayeeyah! — Damn! I thought. *Who is this woman?* I glared at her, but said nothing more, as I leaned over and untied Bik's leash. I wove its end among my fingers.

I noticed that the woman carried a folded copy of one of Shanghai's White Russian-language newspapers, *Slovo — The Word —* under her arm.

Was she one of those leftist radicals causing chaos in our streets? I wondered.

I smiled. "Come with us," I said to the young woman, as I straightened up. "Come with me and my dog. We can get her water over at the Blossom Café on Kiangse Road, while you and I have some refreshments and talk. You will be my guest."

"*Spasibo — Thank you*" she said in Russian, as she nodded.

I noted that she didn't smile although she accepted my invitation. I also noted that although she'd said *Thank you* in Russian, she didn't look like one of those White Russian refugees our city has been inundated with. She appeared to be Chinese.

"You're speaking Russian? Yet you look Chinese," I said.

"I am Chinese," she said, "but I speak Russian."

We settled at an outside table and formally introduced ourselves. I told her my name. Her name was Wu Mei-hua, meaning *Beautiful Flower*. We ordered two bottles of *Ewo* beer, smoked my *Three Cats* cigarettes, and gave Bik a dish filled with water.

We ate, drank, smoked, and talked for more than two hours. We had nothing in common, it seemed, other than our mutual interest in currently learning about one another and our shared interest in Bik.

I told her I was a former SMP policeman, now working privately as a detective. She told me that up until a few years ago she'd been a university student; that she had studied for a time in Moscow (thus her ability to read and speak Russian); that she had several advanced degrees; and that she once had been an active member of the Communist Youth movement, but had since retired from politics.

Bik sat at her feet the whole time we talked. The young woman stroked Bik's head and back as we learned about one another.

I told her a bit about my family, especially about my Elder Brother, Sun-yu. Mei-hua told me that her father was a high-ranking officer in the KMT, and that she now was a bored civilian employed by the KMT, who did not trust her because of her history, so gave her few assignments to perform.

I thought this was ironic work for a formerly active CCP Youth Movement member, but didn't say so since I only knew the woman casually. But I wondered why she would accept such a role, given her political history she'd described to me.

"So you no longer are a Communist?" I said.

"*Da* — *Yes,* and, *Nyet* — *No.* I no longer am anything political. I am struggling with that conflict," she said. "Does this matter to you, if I am or am not?"

I shook my head and shrugged my shoulders.

"Yes," I said. "I mean, no. Not a bit, I think. I just find it interesting. You're the first Communist I've ever met. At least as far as I know. Anyway, to answer your question, I'm not sure."

We exchanged telephone numbers and promised to get together again soon.

CHAPTER 11

THE PAST: 1929

HER NAME HAD NOT ALWAYS been the Yellow Swan. Not when she was growing up in Peking, the only child of a Chinese mother and Japanese father. And not on the day she moved from Peking to Shanghai to begin her career as a chanteuse.

Her birth name was Matsuko— Pine Tree — a name chosen by her father to reflect her parents' wish that their daughter live a long and stable life.

Matsuko Akasuki's life changed in 1918, two days after her seventh birthday, when her mother was mysteriously strangled to death. The killer was never found.

From that time forward, her father insisted that Matsuko discard the Taoist life her mother had taught her to follow, and insisted that she thereafter follow the unwritten code of the Samurai — the Bushido Code — and that she live by Bushido's Eight Virtues of Righteousness, Loyalty, Courage, Honor, Benevolence, Sincerity, Self-Control, and Respect.

"*Hai!*" her father had said to her. "Your mother is no longer here to indulge you, Matsuko." This was the day after her mother's funeral. "I will now see to it that you grow up as a proper Nipponese woman, even though we both are stuck in this wretched land."

As time passed, as Matsuko entered and then grew beyond her teen years, her father became increasingly distant, even cold, talking to his daughter only when it was necessary for him to reprimand her for having strayed from one or more of the Eight Virtues.

Unfortunately, Matsuko's life after her mother died became hard in other ways, too. The same week as her mother's funeral, her father removed Matsuko from the Chinese school her mother had sent her to, and enrolled her in one of Peking's Japanese schools. There, Matsuko's fellow students teased her because she was not full-blooded Japanese, refused to include her as one of their friends for the same reason, and generally tormented her either by taunting her about her mixed-blood status or by ignoring her altogether.

Matsuko responded by inwardly becoming — in her own mind and in the eyes of her father — more Japanese than were her full-blooded classmates, as she voraciously studied the Way of Bushido and embraced its code.

As a good Bushido student, Matsuko revered the Mikado — the Emperor, the Sun God, the heavenly sovereign of the Land of the Rising Sun.

As a result of this adoration, and to further understand her Japanese heritage, Matsuko studied the history of Japan, and memorized its geography, culture, and politics. By the time she was twenty years old, Matsuko's father had come to revere her, and at long last warmed to her, constantly complementing her on her mastery of the Eight Virtues.

In her father's eyes, Matsuko had finally learned, and was successfully practicing, the Way of Bushido.

There was, however, one anomaly in Matsuko's life.

In addition to the Emperor, and all he represented, Matsuko had two other loves in her life. She loved music and she secretly loved a young Yakuza assassin named Kanji Gorō.

Curiously, Matsuko did not love Japanese music. Nor did she care for the Chinese music her mother had played on a lute for her when Matsuko was a young girl.

The music Matsuko loved was American music. Specifically, American jazz and Broadway show tunes, the hot music of the 1920s she'd heard over the radio and had heard in an American-operated department store — the Yankee Emporium — when she worked there as a student bookkeeper one summer while school was in recess.

This music, and Kanji-san, were Matsuko's escape from her harsh, Bushido life.

Eventually, using her knowledge of American music, Matsuko taught herself to sing it as if she were a westerner, an American, although she did not then know the meanings of the words she sang.

CHAPTER 12

DAY ONE OF THE INVESTIGATION

HEARD THE CRACKLING OF THE overhead electric wires and the screech of metal wheels on steel tracks before I ever saw the streetcar round the corner and head toward me.

I left Bik and hopped aboard the trolley as it slowed down for me, then rode it over to the Bund. I could see the Cathay Hotel as I stepped down from the trolley's retractable steel steps into the muddy street.

As usual, the Bund was alive with automobiles, trucks, horses, carriages, and other streetcars, all of which competed with the flowing wave of rickshaws, pedestrians, and bicycles for control of the avenue.

I stepped onto the sidewalk and headed toward 20 Nanking Road, the Cathay's entrance's street address. I walked slowly, joining the many *Amahs* who pushed foreign babies in their strollers, all of us dodging every manner of two-wheeled vehicle and blindly-rushing pedestrians, as we made our way forward.

I stopped in front of the hotel, looked up, and admired its edifice, before walking up to its entrance.

The Cathay Hotel, although opened by Victor Sassoon in 1929, has remained one of Shanghai's most luxurious hotels.

It competes favorably with the newer and taller Park Hotel, as well as with the older, but much more imposing, Astor House, among some of the Settlement's most luxurious hotels still standing.

As I walked up to the entrance, I realized I'd never been inside the building, although I have walked by it, or ridden past it, hundreds of times. It was not a place we Chinese were readily welcomed, although by law no hotel could turn us away if we insisted on entering and using its facilities. Few of us ever did.

Almost everything I knew about the hotel I've learned over the years from various stories in newspapers, including information and rumors from their gossip columns.

That was how I learned, for example, that it was here in the Cathay Hotel that Noel Coward, while sitting up in bed recovering from a bout of flu, wrote the first draft of his famous stage play, *Private Lives,* in just four days. And it was in the Cathay, too, that the movie stars Charlie Chaplin and Paulette Goddard had recently dined at the hotel's Dragon Phoenix restaurant, and that Douglas Fairbanks, the American film idol, had recently danced in the ballroom on each of the nine nights he stayed in the hotel, dancing with a different flower-seller girl he'd brought with him each evening.

I knew I would never see the most celebrated aspects of the hotel — the reputedly magnificent eighth-floor ballroom or any of the hotel's five restaurants — since I could never afford to throw away my hard-earned money in those places, much as I might want to do so just one time for the experience. These places were off-limits to a person like me who operated on a frugal budget.

I stepped through the hotel's ornate entrance into the lobby and looked around. I was impressed.

I first noticed that the lobby's air seemed much cooler and fresher than the air outside where the street absorbed the humidity that drifted up from the Whangpoo River and Soochow Creek. This, as I had read somewhere, undoubtedly was the result of the hotel's special cooling system in which incoming air was washed in a spray of iced, atomized water, keeping the temperature in the lobby agreeable on even the most humid days outside.

The other thing I noticed was the presence of the much-advertised and flaunted glassware created by the French artisan, René Lalique. It seemed to be everywhere — hanging from walls, sitting in the center of tables that were scattered around the lobby, and placed in the middle of two large fountains located on the far side of the large room.

As I entered, I looked across the lobby and saw the famous Horse and Hounds Bar where, it has been written, Victor Sassoon often could be seen talking with guests and pouring them free pink-champagne drinks. Given my history with him, I was happy Sassoon was not there this morning.

I left the entranceway and walked deeper into the lobby.

I knew I could not just stroll up to management, introduce myself as a private investigator, and ask to visit the crime scene and to talk to potential witnesses. That would destroy my cover. Instead, I would have to approach this deviously, adapting my methods to circumstances as they arose.

I stopped walking and looked around. I didn't see anyone I recognized. No one on the hotel's staff seemed to be paying any attention to me. Taking advantage of this, I strode over to the bank of three lifts, and rode one from the lobby level to the ninth-floor Tower Club.

CHAPTER 13

THE RECENT PAST: 1936

Sixty-two year old KMT Colonel Wu Lin-feng stood at attention facing his superior officer, a general who Lin-feng hoped one day to replace as a senior officer in Chiang's KMT army.

"*Heya — My friend,*" the general said. "Your career is again at risk because of your daughter. Questions are being asked about your loyalty because of her past political activities."

Lin-feng stiffened. *Doesn't the past ever go away?* he thought.

He'd heard this before, too many times to be shocked by it, but he was unsettled, nonetheless, for the implicit danger it posed to him and his family. The mere fact that this was again being talked about by his superiors carried peril with it.

Lin-feng had long been aware that some superior officers — some as eminent in the army as Generalissimo Chiang Kai-shek, himself — from time-to-time had questioned his loyalty and, rumor said, had suppressed his promotion to general because his daughter had been an active participant in the enemy-CCP's movement against the Republic.

Some people in high places, he'd learned, too, had even speculated publicly that Mei-hua was a Communist. It was even rumored that she had participated in the Long March until she became ill, had dropped out, had convalesced with a peasant family, and then eventually had returned home.

"I don't know if your daughter still is active with the enemy," the general said, "but for your own good, Lin-feng, you must cause her to cleanse her stained reputation.

"She must perform a public act of recantation of her leftist views and rumored activities on behalf of the bandits. Otherwise, my friend, who knows what might become of your career."

Lin-feng thought about this. Mei-hua no longer was active in CCP affairs, and now she even worked for the KMT in a civilian capacity. But he knew her well enough not to expect her to agree to perform a public recantation, no matter how much he might plead with her to do so. Mei-hua was too proud to stand in a public forum and speak the words that would erase her prior beliefs and actions, even if doing so would protect him and the rest of their family.

Perhaps there is another way, he thought.

He knew this would not be an easy task, but perhaps he could persuade Mei-hua to send a written statement to a newspaper admitting she'd once been a CCP member and had engaged in anti-state activities when she was naïve and young. She also would have to write that she has since come to her senses and has severed all connections with the bandits.

This format, he hoped, would not humiliate her as much as a public, oral retraction might do. She might be amenable, he hoped, to sending such a benign letter to a newspaper in order to aid her family.

As he thought about what the general said — even the fact that he was saying this at all, warning him, in effect — Lin-feng relaxed. His superior's words today meant he would not yet be demoted or imprisoned for treason because of Mei-hua. Today's quiet dressing-down by the general — instead of arresting him without warning — was a friendly word of advice only, and he could handle that for now. Today would not be the end of his career, nor the termination of his freedom. His superior officer was alerting him, in his own subtle way, that he again was being looked at by other superior officers. Perhaps for a promotion, he hoped, if he heeded the message of the warning, or, if he did not, perhaps for his termination in the KMT or imprisonment or, in these troubled times, perhaps something even worse.

"I understand, General," Lin-feng said. "I will speak with Mei-hua and arrange for her to recant. She no longer participates in radical activities with the bandits. The sooner the world is made aware of this, the better off we all will be. I will see to this quickly."

CHAPTER 14

DAY ONE OF THE INVESTIGATION

STEPPED OFF THE LIFT INTO a small lobby having a thickly carpeted floor. No one was in sight. I could see a sign over the Tower Club's entryway down the hallway. The club's entrance was blocked by a pair of closed glass doors. It was too early in the day for the club to be hosting patrons. That would not occur until around 9:00 p.m. or, perhaps, even later.

I walked over and tried one of the doors. It was locked. I looked around. I was alone.

I quickly attacked the door's lock with my lock-picking tools, and easily gained entrance to the darkened club's main entertaining room.

Much to my surprise, based on the club's fame, purported modernity, and its reputed popularity, the entertaining room the club occupied was small, about the same size as a typical, older basement jazz club in the French Concession.

I walked across the parquet-wood floor to the small stage. It had a dark curtain that served as a backdrop. I looked behind the curtain and saw that it covered the entrance to a corridor leading away from the stage and entertaining room. I hoped the corridor would be where I would find the Yellow Swan's changing room.

I'd just taken a few steps when someone called out to me.

"Hey! I say, you there, Mate, what are you doing here? The club's closed until tonight. No one's allowed in the club this early, and never backstage."

I turned around and saw a young, Round-Eyes, white pageboy walking toward me. He was probably eighteen or nineteen years old. He was dressed in a burgundy uniform having gold twine shoulder braids, a pillbox hat with a tie-string under his chin, a brass-button jacket, and flared-at-the-cuffs dress slacks. He shuffled silently, but swiftly, over the carpet toward me.

"*Heya! — Hello!*" I said, making eye contact with him, smiling as I spoke. "I was looking for the Yellow Swan's changing room. I'm a devoted fan of hers. That is, I was a devoted fan before she tragically died. I wanted to see where it happened, I'm so saddened by her death." I slowly lowered my eyes and head to lend authenticity to my lie.

"There's nothing to see anymore," the pageboy said. "The room is empty now. I'm told it won't be used again as a changing room, in her honor, but from now on will be for storage."

I decided to try one of the interrogation techniques I often successfully employed when I was a member of the SMP Special Branch interrogation squad. I feigned confusion. This, in my experience, was a better way of initially obtaining information from another person than by showing open curiosity and asking specific questions.

"*Ayeeyah!*" I said, pouting as I did so. "I don't understand." I frowned and slowly shook my head in despair.

"Why would the hotel close up the room and not honor her

memory. The Yellow Swan was a great performer. Will they at least nail up a plaque by the door in her honor?" I opened my eyes wide to show hope and expectation.

The pageboy responded as I hoped he would. He broke into a big smile. I knew I now had a co-conspirator in my desire to honor the Yellow Swan.

"I also was a great fan," he said, "and I, like you, Mate, will miss her dearly." He paused and gazed up the hallway as if remembering something pleasant he hadn't yet shared with me.

He continued, as he pointed to the curtain at the end of the corridor.

"I used to stand behind that curtain when she performed her sets, listening to her sing. She brought great joy into my life, she did."

I nodded my understanding, but said nothing, not wanting to break the spell the young man had just initiated.

Seconds ticked by. Neither of us spoke. I found it easy to remain silent. Long experience had shown me that silence is an effective interviewing technique, often inspiring the other person to speak just to fill-in the gap caused by the silence. It worked this time, too.

"Would you like to peek into her changing room, even though it's empty now?" the pageboy said. "You can still feel her presence. I mean, at least I do when I go in there."

"You go in there?" I said, trying to make my voice sound both astonished and envious. "You're so lucky to do that."

The pageboy smiled and nodded. "You bet I do. You can go in there, too, if you want. I can let you do that if you won't stay too long. I don't want to get into no trouble. I have to get back to my station in the lobby."

"*Ah! Shi — Yes,*" I said. "That would be thrilling." I broke into a wide grin and nodded several times to convince him of my excitement.

"You honor me by allowing me this special treat. I'll owe you," I said, as I slowly bowed my head.

"Follow me, then," he said, squaring his shoulders as he pulled a key ring from his back pocket and led me along the corridor to the Yellow Swan's changing room.

He opened the door, and I stepped into the crime scene.

CHAPTER 15

THE PRESENT: 1937

KANJI GORŌ SAT IN THE gloom that blanketed the inside of a brick facade and straw-roof hut located in Shanghai's Hongkew district. The hut had been loaned to him since 1934 by a local Yakuza member who no longer used it.

Kanji thought over his plan for finding Matsuko's killer and achieving his revenge. He sat crossed-legged on a thick tatami mat, in front of a single clay pot that contained burning oil and incense. He was naked. He faced a full-length mirror that leaned against one wall. He stared at the reflection of his oiled, muscular body.

Like most of his Yakuza brethren, Kanji had decorated his body from his ankles to the base of his neck with *Irezumi* — intricate, colorful tattoos. These designs were created from ink inserted beneath the skin using hand-made needles carved from sharpened bamboo or steel. The procedure was extremely painful, and was seen among the Yakuza as a mark of ones bravery. The designs often took years to complete.

Kanji's inked patterns, which consisted of bright green, red, yellow, blue, and orange designs, looked, at first glance, much like Kitagawa Utamaro's woodblock images of the Floating

World. But unlike Utamaro's well-balanced, carefully composed images, Kanji's tattoos had been severely crowded together and often overlapped one another, so that none of Kanji's ink had the beauty, grace or subtlety of the Floating World's pictorial art Utamaro had created.

After thirty minutes passed, Kanji stood, put out the incense pot, and toweled the oil off his body. He dressed himself in common street cloths, fully covering himself up to his neck so that none of his ink showed to the outside world.

He was ready to begin his search for Matsuko's killer.

CHAPTER 16

DAY ONE OF THE INVESTIGATION

A s I stepped into the Yellow Swan's changing room, I turned back to the pageboy who was standing in the hallway, close by the entry door, seemingly waiting to follow me in. He peered beyond me into the empty room as if this time he expected to see someone or something in there he hadn't seen before.

"*Ayeeyah,*" I said. "I'll close the door for a few minutes, if you don't mind. I would like to be alone with the Yellow Swan's memory for a short while."

I nodded gravely at him as I said this, trying to subtly suggest that my decision to exclude him, although a reluctant decision by me, was a normal, expected outcome for any true fan under the circumstances.

"But—"

He started to say something, probably to protest, but I didn't give him the chance to complete his objection. I gently closed the door, nodding solemnly at him as I did so, saying, just before I lost sight of him, "Thank you, my friend. You, too, are a true fan of the Yellow Swan."

I turned on the ceiling light, then walked the room's small perimeter. I used my pocket-size electric torch to see into corners and crevices. I hoped I might find something missed in the emptying and cleaning of the room. There was nothing.

I opened a stand-alone A-Frame wardrobe — the only furniture in the room — and shined my torch into it. I found nothing. It, like the room itself, had been emptied. I looked in the commode, but again found nothing. The pageboy had been correct. The room, as he'd said, was empty. My visit to the Yellow Swan's changing room yielded no information to me.

I completed my inspection, which was not difficult to do since the room was empty. I did not want the pageboy — if he still was outside the changing room — to become impatient with the amount of time I spent there and ask me to leave. That might arouse suspicion in him that my motive for being there was not as benign as I had pretended, that I was not a lonely, sad fan who wanted to commune with, and have one last memory of, our shared idol, but that I'd had some other, unstated, motive in coming here. I wanted to stay on his good side for when I would come back to the hotel and question him and other employees at some later time this week.

He was nowhere to be seen when I stepped out into the hallway, so I walked back to the lift and rode it down to the lobby.

As I stepped out of the lift, I saw a familiar man heading toward me. It was Akio Harue, the Dwarf Bandit who worked in the Hongkew section of the Settlement as an inspector detective for the JMP. Our paths had crossed two years ago when I was working the flower-seller girls' murder cases. The experience had not been pleasant for me.

What's he doing here? I wondered, suddenly feeling vulnerable. *This isn't part of his jurisdiction.*

Our eyes met briefly, but, as far as I could tell, he hadn't noticed me. Or, if he had, he didn't recognize me. My presence in the hotel's lobby hadn't alerted him that something unusual was going on. I quickly looked away from him to avoid calling attention to myself.

Before he passed the halfway point in the lobby, heading toward me, I stepped back into the lift, closed the door, and rode it up to the second floor. When the doors opened, I walked out into an empty corridor lined with closed entrance doors for several businesses. I waited in the empty hallway, hoping that none of the office doors would open and discharge a worker who might question my presence there.

I waited a while to give Harue time to leave the lobby and, hopefully, go to some other floor. I hoped he would not remain downstairs or step out of the lift into the second floor corridor while I still was here. When ten minutes passed, I rode the lift back to the lobby. I looked around for Harue, but didn't see him.

I hurried across the room and left the hotel. I jumped into a taxi and rode it back to my office.

CHAPTER 17

DAY ONE OF THE INVESTIGATION

HAVING LEARNED NOTHING USEFUL AT the Cathay Hotel crime scene, I went looking for some of the reliable informants I'd often turned to as sources in my two years as a PI. I hoped one of them might have heard something about the homicide that would help me.

I had used some of these same people when I was a Special Branch inspector detective, sometimes trading information from them for their freedom, sometimes merely looking the other way when I caught them in some infraction in return for future information from them, and sometimes by coming up with *yuan* — *cash* — to compensate them for their information.

Because I no longer was part of the SMP, I didn't have the implicit, coercive power to arrest or release an informant, so now I probably would have to pay cash for any information they might offer me. This would not be as easy as it might sound. I would have to bankroll the payments from my own meager funds.

But, I realized, I also might be able to obtain information from these men and women in return for anticipated favors to be delivered by me sometime in the future. I would promise to share information with them that I might learn during my unrelated PI investigations, so that they could, in turn, sell that information to their own contacts. I also, as an alternative barter, would promise to investigate their future jams with the police for them, without charge, and to turn the information I found out over to their barristers to help with their future cases.

I started by meeting with my most reliable source, a small-time triad member named Zhu Chan.

I first met Zhu after I arrested him on three occasions for shop lifting, selling opium, and for soliciting sexual favors from a ten year old girl. On each occasion, Zhu paid his fine and quickly returned to the streets. Such is the power and influence of the triads, even for such a minor member as Zhu.

On another occasion, when I still was a uniformed constable, I took Zhu into custody when he attempted to rob a tourist late at night as the tourist and his flower-seller-girl companion exited the Venus Café, one of Shanghai's most popular cabarets, located in the Old City.

I allowed the flower-seller girl to leave the arrest scene since she was merely earning her living and still had a full night's work ahead of her. But not so for Zhu. Instead of taking him to the station house to process, as the regulations required, I took him behind the Venus Café, and offered him a deal.

"*Ayeeyah*! Why aren't you taking me to the precinct, Constable," Zhu said, as we settled in behind the cabaret. He squinted at me with suspicious, skeptical eyes.

"Are you going to beat me first? Well, so be it," he said, as he shrugged his shoulders, seemingly resolved to his fate. "Let's get it over with."

"No beating, Zhu. Just an opportunity for you," I said. I removed the handcuffs from his wrists.

He looked puzzled. He stiffened, on his guard, probably suspicious of my motives.

"What are you talking about? Take me to the station house so my brothers can arrange to free me."

"If I have to take you in," I said, "I'll also let it be known to everyone that you've cooperated with me on many occasions as my private informant. Your triad brothers will find that interesting, I suspect."

Zhu's face darkened. "*Ayeeyah! — Damn you!* Why would you do that? I have never helped you."

"Your triad brothers won't know that, will they? They'll take the safe route and will believe me.

"So, Zhu," I said, "from now on you *will* help me. Otherwise, I'll let slip information that will not please your brothers when they hear it."

And so Zhu became my informant. To my surprise, he turned out to be reliable, although expensive.

I arranged to meet Zhu at the Fong Kee Cafe on Avenue Foch in the French Concession. We avoided using the outdoor patio seating, and settled instead at a table inside so as not to be readily seen together should someone happen past who knew either of us.

As always, we skipped the introductory greetings required by Confucian and Taoist rituals. We were there to do business.

"What have you heard about the death of the woman known as the Yellow Swan?" I said.

Zhu raised one shoulder in a mild, indifferent shrug. "They

say she was well-liked as a singer and available as a customer for opium and cocaine."

"What do you know about who killed her or why?"

"Nothing."

I believed him. As far as I knew, Zhu had never lied to me. When he had information, he came out with it. When he did not have information, he got to the point and said so. He did not make up things and sell me phony information.

"I want you to find out what you can and get back to me fast. I don't have much time to solve this," I said.

"*Ayeeyah!* I cannot do that, not this time. So sorry."

"What do you mean you can't—"

"*Dui bu qi. — Sorry.* The word had been put out that no one is to touch this crime. No one is to even speculate out loud who might have committed the murder or why they might have done so. It is to be as if this murder never happened. The Yellow Swan is to be just a vague memory to everyone. I cannot help you this time."

That stopped me. "What are you talking about, Zhu? Who would require such a thing?"

He didn't answer right away. He stared at me for a few seconds, flicked an imaginary piece of dirt from his sleeve, then nodded his head, and said, "Big-Eared Tu. But I never told you this. Tu has spread the word that this crime never happened, and so it has not."

Over the next three hours, I met with six other men who were low-level members of triads, and who occasionally served as informants for me. I also met with two flower-seller girls and two madams. They all occasionally sold or traded information to me. Each meeting resulted in the same impasse as had my meeting with Zhu.

My informants were useless to me in this investigation. Big-Eared Tu, for some reason I did not know, had seen to that.

CHAPTER 18

DAY ONE OF THE INVESTIGATION

Although I'd only been involved with the case for less than one full day, I was frustrated by my lack of progress and by the fact that I now had another obstacle to overcome — Tu's prohibition against anyone working the case. I decided to report the situation to Chief Inspector Chapman. This would satisfy his expressed need for involvement, as well as fulfill his direct order to me to keep him informed of my progress.

I hoped my report would cause the chief inspector to see the hopelessness of the situation he, and now Big-Eared Tu, had forced me into. I hoped the chief inspector would ease his requirements that the investigation be concluded within one week and conducted entirely in secret, all without the sharing of information with me by the SMP.

Using the prearranged signal we'd agreed to for me to contact him, I called his office. I disguised my voice by placing my handkerchief over the telephone's mouthpiece.

"*Wu an — Good afternoon.* Chief Inspector Chapman, please," I said to the switchboard operator.

"Chapman, here," he said, a full minute later.

I said only the words we'd agreed upon: "Let's dine." Then I hung up. He knew where to go to find me, and that I would be there one hour after my call to him. No more was necessary from either of us.

We met in a back room at the Willow Pattern Tea House, a structure constructed during the Ming Dynasty. The tea house sat on pilings in the middle of the Whangpoo River.

The Willow Pattern Tea House, being old and subject to ancient and modern superstitions, had bottles arranged along the edges of its roof, each with its open neck facing outward, ready to catch any demons who might want to fly down and enter the building. In addition, as further protection against the evil spirits we Chinese know exist, the tea house's long, wooden-entrance walkway — called the Bridge of Nine Turnings — which led from the river's bank, over the water, to the entrance of the tea house, sharply zig-zagged left to right and back again, nine times, to keep out evil spirits who, as everyone knows, prefer to travel in a straight line.

"Good of you to keep me up to date, Old Boy. Just what I wanted," Chapman said, once we settled into a private room at the back end of the tea house. He nodded, smiled, and puffed his pipe.

I waited until a pot of tea and two cups had been set down between us, and until the attendant left, before I spoke.

"My report, sir, is that I have nothing positive to report."

Chapman frowned and stiffened. He squeezed his pipe in his left hand until his knuckles whitened.

He then tried to make the best of the situation. "That's not good, Sun-jin. Not good at all. Not what I expected from you."

He puffed his pipe again. "I anticipated more from you, even this early in your investigation." He sighed and slowly shook his head.

"Oh, well," he said, using a tone of voice that suggested he was resigned to the challenges of the situation he had placed me in. "Perhaps it's too soon to expect more." He nodded as if confirming this belief for himself.

"Chief Inspector," I said. "I'm finding the restrictions you've placed on me too limiting. I don't think I can make progress and solve the crime in the time allowed under all your conditions. My experience tells me it's an impossible situation."

"You don't have a choice, Sun-jin." He sniffed and winced as if he'd suddenly smelled something foul.

I shrugged. I decided to bluff. I had nothing to lose.

"Well, sir, I can just give up now and let the SMP officer you've assigned to the case do his work. I don't think I have any other choice."

Chapman shook his head. He smiled a smile that was meant, I think, to reassure me that we were on the same side in this difficult situation. His smile was cold. It did not reassure me.

"Sun-jin," he said, speaking warmly now, "I know the working circumstances are not ideal, not the conditions you were used to when you were with the Special Branch, but we have no other alternative. I already explained that to you."

He raised his eyebrows as if to reassure me that he was sincere in his sympathy for me.

"Besides, Old Boy, consider this. As I said, it is only the first day of your investigation. Things are bound to get better."

I slowly shook my head, as if I were resigned to accepting his explanation, as if I had never considered this aspect of my state of affairs and had not already rejected it. As if him saying this to me now made it so, and thereby resolved my concern.

I dropped the point and decided to give him an actual report.

"Well, then, sir, I should tell you what I've done so far.

I described my unsuccessful attempt to find other cases of performers who had been murdered lately to see if any of those crimes were linked to the death of the Yellow Swan.

I told him about my conversation with Zhu Chan (although I did not reveal Zhu's name) and with my other informants. I repeated Zhu's information that Big-Eared Tu had put the word out on the street that the murder had not occurred.

The chief inspector understood the implication of this for my investigation.

"I think I need to visit Tu," I said. "I need to convince him to stop blocking the investigation."

"No," Chapman said. "No outsiders. I told you that. It's too risky. You shouldn't have approached informants either."

I let this pass.

I then described my visit to the Cathay Hotel, to the Tower Club, and, specifically, to the Yellow Swan's changing room.

I concluded by saying, "And here's an interesting situation that came up as I was leaving the hotel, one I hadn't anticipated. When I stepped off the lift, I saw JMP Inspector Detective Harue walking across the lobby, heading my way. You remember him, don't you?"

Chapman nodded, but said nothing. He squinted as if the lights in our room had suddenly become bright.

"What was he doing there?" I asked. "The Settlement, outside Hongkew. It isn't his jurisdiction."

"I don't know," Chapman said. He frowned. "Perhaps he's

representing the JMP in the investigation. After all, the Yellow Swan was part Jap."

I shook my head as if disgusted by the situation, which I was, as I again recalled how Harue and I had been at each other's throats two years ago.

"He better stay out of my way," I said, "if you want to keep our investigation secret and meet your timetable. Otherwise, he might blow this whole thing open or, at least, slow down our progress. I don't need to deal with him as a distraction."

"No," the chief inspector said, slowly shaking his head, "just the opposite, Old Boy."

His eyes narrowed and he looked hard at me. "You better stay out of *his* way. He likely has an official right to be involved. You don't."

I reluctantly nodded. I knew he was correct.

"Like I said, sir, Harue could be a problem."

The chief inspector didn't bite. Instead, he said, "You better figure out a way to avoid him and to quickly wrap up this case. Otherwise, both Shanghai and you might have more to worry about than Inspector Detective Harue and the JMP."

CHAPTER 19

THE PAST: 1934
PEKING

MATSUKO WAS COMPLETING HER SECOND vocal set of the evening at the Double-Dragon Club in the Badlands section of Peking when she noticed a thin, mustached, Round-Eyes white man, in his middle to late fifties, smiling at her from a table near the stage. He nodded once as their eyes made brief contact, then he turned back to his drink.

His table was set for two places, but he sat alone.

Although the Round-Eyes seemed to be watching her closely, he did not stare at Matsuko the way most men who looked at her stared — admiring her and, likely, coveting her beauty and young sexuality. This man's eyes drilled through her with an intensity Matsuko hadn't experienced before. His stare set her nerves on edge.

She finished singing the set.

"*Hai!*" she said, speaking Japanese, rather than Mandarin, to this mostly Nipponese audience. "*Arigatou Gozaimasu — Thank you.*" She smiled warmly.

"Thank you, ladies and gentlemen," she said, now speaking

in Mandarin for the few Chinese in the audience. She bowed and prepared to walk off the stage.

"I am so happy to sing popular American songs for you," she said. She bowed again. Then she furtively glanced at the Round-Eyes sitting in front of her.

As their eyes met, the man slowly shook his head no, and summoned Matsuko to his table, using his index finger.

Matsuko frowned. *Who is this Round-Eyes who thinks he can order me to come to his table?* She abruptly turned away and left the stage. She did not look back.

As she approached her changing room, after she'd stopped to speak with the Double-Dragon Club's manager, one of the club's pageboys handed her a note. Matsuko barely glanced at the folded paper. She carried it, unopened, into her changing room and dropped it onto her makeup table.

She sat down, glanced at her face in the mirror, then toweled herself off, drying her face and forehead. She added some fresh makeup to her face and eyes and some rouge to her lips to repair the damage done by the stage's hot flood lights. Then she opened and read the note she'd received.

The man stood up and smiled as Matsuko approached his table. She noticed he used a cane to leverage himself up from his chair.

He bowed slightly, then walked around the table to the other side and pulled out the spare chair for her.

As he returned to his seat, he said, "Do you drink champagne, Miss Akasuki?" He spoke with a slight British accent that blended with some other accent Matsuko hadn't heard before and couldn't place.

Before Matsuko could answer, the man raised his arm and waived over a waiter. "A bottle of Bollinger La Grande Annee Brut," he said. "Make it 1928." He turned back to Matsuko, and smiled.

Matsuko trembled slightly, awed by the man's self-confidence. The Round-Eyes exuded wealth, understated power, and expectation. Matsuko remained quiet.

The man looked across the table at Matsuko, smiled once more, and softly said, "My name is Victor Sassoon. I live in Shanghai."

Matsuko returned his smile, barely masking her trepidation. Her eyes darted around the room, unable to fix themselves on the man's face.

What does he want with me? Is he a Round-Eyes on the prowl for a young Oriental woman?

"*Heya — Hello,*" she finally said, at first speaking Mandarin, then immediately switching to English, as the man had addressed her, still smiling as she spoke.

"Please, sir," she said. "I do not speak good English. We may talk in Japanese or Mandarin, if you please."

Sassoon nodded. "Mandarin's fine."

"My name, sir, as you likely know from the club's poster out front, is Matsuko Akasuki. I am happily pleased to meet with you, Mr. Sassoon." She demurely, slowly, lowered her eyelids before looking up at him again.

Sassoon nodded again. "I hope tonight to cause the club's management to permanently replace that poster out front," he said, "to render it obsolete."

Matsuko was puzzled. She bit her lower lip. "Please explain, sir. Replace poster? Why? Am I being fired? What do you mean, obsolete?"

Sassoon did not answer. Instead, he raised his champagne flute in a toast, and said, "Here's to doing business together, Miss Akasuki." He sipped his drink.

Matsuko frowned, more puzzled than upset. She took a sip of her drink. She stared at Sassoon, and waited. She had no idea what to say to this Round-Eyes because she had no idea what he was talking about. She wished her father was present so she could consult with him.

"As I said," Sassoon continued, "I live in Shanghai. I am the owner of a hotel there. It is the most luxurious and the most modern hotel in all China. I call it the Cathay Hotel."

Matsuko continued staring at the stranger over the lip of her glass. She remained silent.

"As part of the Cathay's entertainment, I operate a nightclub in the tower on the ninth floor. The Tower Club features an American jazz band from Kansas City. I want it now to also feature a girl singer, and I want you to be that girl."

Matsuko took a few seconds to reply. "*Qing — Please.* I am truly flattered, sir, but I cannot accept your kind offer. I know no one in Shanghai.

"My family, such as it is, lives here in Peking, and I have a good job here at the Double-Dragon. Giving all that up to try to advance myself would be bad *joss* — bad *luck*. I will not tempt the gods to punish me for my haughtiness and ambition."

"That's nonsense," Sassoon said, an edge creeping into his voice. "I will pay you very well, Miss Akasuki. Extremely well. You shouldn't make a rash decision you will later regret."

Matsuko shook her head no, but said nothing else.

Sassoon shifted in his chair. He took a deep breath to calm his rising anger. He was not used to being rebuffed when he was being generous. He deliberately softened his voice.

"Miss Akasuki, I will turn you into a star, into the most famous woman in all China," he said, his tone suggesting full confidence he could do so. "More famous even than Madam Chiang Kai-shek."

Sassoon watched Matsuko's eyes widen as she absorbed this statement. Now he was getting somewhere.

"*Kenong — Maybe*," Matsuko said, speaking softly, as if talking to herself. For the first time since she joined him at his table, she looked directly into Sassoon's eyes and smiled.

Sassoon refilled his flute. A nearby waiter took a step toward the table to take over the task of pouring drinks, but Sassoon held up his palm and stopped him. Sassoon turned back toward Matsuko and held up the bottle to silently ask if she would like a refill. She shook her head no.

"*Qing — Please*," she said. "You will explain to me what you mean?"

Sassoon slowly, very deliberately, placed the champagne bottle back in the bucket, ignoring Matsuko as if she weren't there. He allowed several seconds to pass before he looked at her again.

"I will make you into a star of the stage, a sensation of the cabaret, in Shanghai. As part of that, I give you a written, legal contract that will be binding on me for two years, but binding on you only for six months. You will perform at the Tower Club as its featured girl singer.

"Any time after six months, if you wish, you may end the contract and quit the club without any penalty for doing so. I, however, will not be permitted to end your contract for the entire two years.

"If you quit, I will move you back to Peking, or to anywhere else in China you want to go, at my expense."

"*Ayeeyah.* You can make me be a singer star?"

"I can, and I will, if you strictly follow my instructions. It's guaranteed."

Matsuko smiled. "*Shi - Yes,* It is good *joss.*"

Sassoon knew then that he had her.

"I return to Shanghai the day after tomorrow, Miss Akasuki. I will need your decision and the signed contract, if we are to do business together, no later than tomorrow by noon."

They met the next morning at the Way of the Pomegranate Inn on Moon Blossom Avenue, in one of Peking's wealthy commercial neighborhoods.

"I have decided to become a star," Matsuko said to Sassoon, again speaking in Mandarin, as soon as they sat.

"Fine. I have the contract with me in anticipation of your good sense," he said. "It is written in Mandarin." He opened the briefcase he'd carried into the inn with him.

Matsuko signed the document without reading it.

"Have you been to Shanghai before?"

Matsuko shook her head.

"I will arrange to have an apartment available to you in the Broadway Mansions Apartments. It is my residential hotel/apartment building, near the Garden Bridge, overlooking the public gardens where Soochow Creek and the Whangpoo River meet.

"You will like it," he said. "It has a beautiful rooftop garden and its own bakery. Your apartment will have a view of the river and of the beautiful skyline along the Bund, across the water."

Matsuko politely smiled, as if what he said actually meant

something to her. "Tell me more, sir, about this place I will live," Matsuko said, "so I can tell it to my father."

Sassoon smiled for the first time since they'd gotten together.

"Broadway Mansions is the tallest and most deluxe apartment-residence in Hongkew. That's the district in Shanghai, in the International Settlement, where you will be required to live because of your Japanese ancestry."

Matsuko nodded, unfazed by his statement. She was well-used to the restrictions the Chinese placed on the Japanese in Peking, so why not in Shanghai, too.

It couldn't be worse in Shanghai, she thought, *perhaps better, where no one will know I am of mixed blood — low faan.*

"There is one condition, however," Sassoon said. "I doubt it should bother you."

Matsuko frowned. She slightly bowed her head in anticipation of what that condition might be, and also as a gesture of respect and good will. She hoped the condition would not be one that would cause her to change her mind about taking the opportunity the Round-Eyes had offered her.

"As part of taking you along the way to stardom, I require that you be mysterious. I need the public to crave information about you — about your age, your origins, and about your personal and family histories. Above all else, I want your public to hunger to know your real name.

"All of that," he said, "and your lovely voice and stage presence, will sell tables at the Tower Club and will take you to stardom."

He paused to see her reaction.

She wrinkled her forehead as if confused.

"You will play to this desire by your fans to know more about you," he said, "even as my public relations people drive your fans to lust after this knowledge. Can you do that? It will be good for business, good for our business together."

Matsuko nodded, even as she wondered what she might have just agreed to participate in.

"If I cannot use my true name," she said, "what am I to be called?"

"Because of your exquisite looks, your beautiful yellow skin, and your long, thin neck, from now on you will be known as the *Yellow Swan*," Sassoon said.

"To all the world, all the time, from the moment you arrive in Shanghai, you will be called the Yellow Swan by everyone, even by me."

CHAPTER 20

THE PRESENT

JMP INSPECTOR DETECTIVE AKIO HARUE stood at attention in front of the Japanese Kwantung colonel's desk. He'd been summoned from his police-barracks in Hongkew to the officer's military encampment at the mouth of the Whangpoo.

The Japanese army and its small fleet of destroyers and gunboats had been keeping vigil over Shanghai from the Whangpoo River ever since the 1932 military incident — referred to by the Chinese as the *January 28 Incident* — when the Kwantung fired upon Chinese students who for weeks had gathered in the Old City to protest Japan's takeover of Manchuria in 1931. These students had implemented a successful boycott of Japanese stores, goods, and services throughout Shanghai. The result of the January 28 Incident was a massacre of protesting students, some bombing of Chapei by Japanese aircraft, and a six-week ongoing battle between the Kwantung and Chinese armies.

"*Hai!* Inspector Detective Harue," the colonel said, speaking Japanese. "You realize, of course, you now are under my command, as are all Japanese Municipal Police employees."

"I have been told that, Colonel."

"I have a mission for you. One that will inestimably aid the Emperor and the cause of the Shōwa Empire in our endeavor to create the Greater East Asia Co-Prosperity Sphere."

Harue fidgeted, but said nothing. He'd been warned months ago by his superior in the JMP that the police department and its daily operations in Shanghai were gradually being undermined and taken over by the military. Harue had known that one day he, too, would be sucked into the maw of that unforgiving, ever metastasizing, elite behemoth called the Kwantung army, and that he would become a puppet of its officers.

"*Hai! — Yes!*, Colonel, he said. I am honored to assist our Emperor's glorious cause." He bowed his head slightly.

Inspector Detective Akio Harue stood just over 1.4 meters — 5'4" — tall. He weighed a little less than 57kg — 126 pounds. He was, like most of his senior colleagues in the JMP, clean shaven except for a dark, pencil-line moustache above his upper lip. His dark bushy eyebrows melded together above his eyes like a single, dark caterpillar.

Harue typically dressed either in an ill-fitting, double-breasted, black wool suit or, in the summer, in an ill-fitting, double-breasted, tan linen suit. He adorned his wide leather belt with a saber he wore on his left side and with a large, 20mm Nambu Taisho 14 Shiki pistol he holstered against his right hip.

Harue detested his posting in Shanghai because he detested the British and Americans, who referred to him as a Jap, and he especially detested the Chinese, who referred to him and to all his countrymen, when they thought he could not hear them, as Dwarf Bandits.

Harue's solace in this situation, as it was for all his colleagues in Shanghai, was their certain knowledge that one day soon the Kwantung army and the local Hongkew Nipponese would rule this city — as the Kwantung army surely would rule all China — subjugating the native Chinese vermin, and also driving out of China the Round-Eyes who had come there as occupiers from Britain, America, France, and elsewhere in the West.

"One of our compatriots has been murdered in this city," the colonel said to Harue. "Her name was Matsuko Akasuki. She was known in Shanghai by her entertainment stage name, the Yellow Swan."

Harue remembered reading about this crime in the local Hongkew Japanese-language newspaper.

"You are to investigate the murder on behalf of the Imperial government," the colonel said.

"*Hai,*" Harue interrupted, "but the crime occurred in the part of the International Settlement that is not Hongkew. The British and American imperialists will never allow us to assert jurisdiction in their Concession."

The colonel abruptly stood up from his desk. His face darkened as he deliberately looked Harue up and down. He shook his head slowly.

"Don't be a damned fool, Harue. We won't ask them to give us permission to participate. We will assert our right to investigate the murder of one of our nationals.

"Then we will — that is, you will — do everything you can to create a military incident. If we must run a parallel investigation, you will do everything in your power to interfere with the SMP's investigation, until you have formulated some basis for an incident.

"Your role will be to cause the murder to ripen into a full-blown situation by finding some important Celestial person to pin the crime on. That will give us reason to march into the balance of the International Settlement, notwithstanding the protests of the British and Americans."

Harue nodded and smiled. "*Hai.*" He put his left hand on the hilt of his saber, clicked his heals together, and nodded again.

Perfect, he thought.

CHAPTER 21

DAY ONE OF THE INVESTIGATION

BECAUSE, RIGHT FROM ITS INCEPTION, my allowable time to solve the Yellow Swan's murder had been curtailed by the chief inspector, and because I could not call on the resources of the SMP to help me offset that disadvantage, I decided to ignore Chapman's order not to involve anyone else in my investigation.

With no firm leads or suspects as yet, and with no help coming to me from my usual informants, thanks to the interference of Big-Eared Tu, I had nothing to lose by seeking the help of others, but much to lose if I did not. That's how I justified my decision to ignore the chief inspector's prohibition against meeting with Tu.

I felt some apprehension at the thought of doing this. Intentionally disobeying Chief Inspector Chapman's instruction not to reveal the existence of my investigation to anyone ran contrary to my beliefs as a Confucian that rules and superiors must be obeyed. Yet, I decided, I had no choice if I were to solve the crime within the chief inspector's onerous timetable.

I would visit Big-Eared Tu to seek his help. Hopefully, my visit to him would inspire him to acknowledge the existence of the crime, and would encourage him to reverse his previous order to have everyone keep hands off the murder. I hoped my personal plea would cause him to use his vast connections throughout Shanghai's underworld to call forth some information that would be useful to me.

I rode the electric streetcar to its stop on Rue Wagner, the tree-lined boulevard in the French Concession where Tu's three-story brick mansion was located.

I looked at Tu's house as I walked up the long, zig-zagging path from the street, toward the front door. His house had been sited on the traditional *Feng Shui* north-south axis, and had the usual raised steps at its entrance to ward off evil spirits.

I saw two watch-towers out front where, I had read somewhere, night watchman, employed by Tu as guards, reputedly struck cymbals each night, beginning at sundown, to scare away evil spirits. They continued this practice throughout the night, doing this for a full minute on each hour until the sun came up in the morning.

I was greeted at the door by the same elderly *Amah* who had admitted me into Tu's home on several occasions two years ago, the last time I came here for help. She led me to the Great Room where Tu was seated. He stood and bowed as I walked over to meet him.

I glanced around as I crossed the Great Room. The sound of Tu's caged lucky crickets and lucky songbirds greeted me as I stepped through the entrance door, but abruptly stopped as my presence in the room became known to them.

It seemed to me that nothing had changed since my last visit. The overall décor still was an uneasy mix of traditional

Confucian furnishings and scholar's artifacts, together with contemporary western Art Deco.

Very, very 1937, I thought.

My overall impression of the Great Room since my last visit hadn't changed either. This was a blend of cultures I would not have expected to find here.

"*Heya! — Hello!*" Tu said. "Welcome again to my home, Mr. Ling." He bowed his head briefly. "You honor me with your presence."

Based on his failure to address me by my former Special Branch title — Inspector Detective — but calling me instead *Mr. Ling*, it was clear Tu knew I no longer was a policeman with the SMP.

"Thank you, Master Tu. I am honored to have you receive me in your home once again. Please call me Sun-jin."

Unlike the last time I visited Tu, that time to request his help in solving a series of homicides in Shanghai's Flowery Kingdom, this time I did not feel intimidated by his presence, his scurrilous notoriety, or his deliberately created and carefully maintained inscrutable persona. I would not be as deferential to him this time as I had been the last several times we met, although I would continue to show him the respect due his station and influence in society. It would be safer for me that way.

Tu bowed his head in the traditional Confucian manner. He brought

his arms up to his chest and then slid each hand up into the wide, opposite sleeve of his purple Mandarin gown. He appeared scholarly and even reposeful, although he was standing, and did not seem menacing, although I knew, he surely was menacing.

We ended the prescribed Confucian and Taoist greeting rituals,

and got down to business.

"I have come once again to ask for your help, Master Tu."

I then gave him information about my investigation that I knew he already knew. For me to act as if he did not already know this information would be dangerous, for it would cause him to lose face. Tu, it was widely said in both official and unofficial police circles, knew everything important — lawful and unlawful — that occurred in Shanghai. His eyes and ears were everywhere.

I described the murder of the Yellow Swan, and the Municipal Council's concern that the Dwarf Bandits might use her homicide as an excuse for a military attack on Shanghai.

"The SMP also is investigating this crime," Tu said. "Why does the chief inspector have you involved?"

I explained my peculiar involvement in the case, holding nothing back. I'd learned two years ago that Tu required nothing less than full candor when dealing with someone.

"The problem for me, Master Tu, is that I must solve this crime within seven days, but must do so without using any of the usual resources of the SMP.

"I would like to be permitted to call upon my usual paid informants, as well as call upon your vast resources throughout Shanghai and all of China, to give me leads to follow. I will be greatly in your debt should you allow me this favor."

Tu narrowed his eyes. "Why would I assist you even if I were able to do so? Why should I care about the death of a half-breed woman?"

I decided to take this on as directly as I could. I'd never

gotten anywhere in the past with Tu when I tip-toed around issues.

"We both know, Master Tu, from events over the past five years, that if the Dwarf Bandits use this murder to manufacture a military incident, your business interests will suffer. It is in your best interest to help me avoid that situation."

Tu offered a slight shrug of one shoulder.

"*Ayeeyah!* I think not. My aid to you could itself be called an incident by the Dwarf Bandits and bring about the potential problem you describe. It is in my self-interest to permit matters to take their own natural course," he said, stating a basic Taoist principle.

"*Wei wu wei*" — *Do not force matters,*" he said, as if I would not have understood what he meant if he had not then explained it to me.

"If I attempt to change the natural course of events, then it is likely the Dwarf Bandits will find some reason to declare the existence of an incident.

"If I do not interfere, and if you do not continue with your investigation, the Dwarf Bandits might not be able to find an excuse to take military action. You — everyone — should show restraint and allow this matter to take its natural course."

I wasn't surprised by Tu's position. It fit his manner of conducting his underworld business, when it suited him to do so, but not when matters did not so suit him. Or so I've been told.

I had hoped to change his mind. I was disappointed.

Tu stood and bowed his head again. Our meeting was over.

Since I already was in the French Concession, I decided to visit my older brother, Ling Sun-yu, who lived and worked there. Even if Tu wouldn't assist me, I knew I would be able to count on Sun-yu to help me if he could. This might be one time when Sun-yu's supposed underworld connections, such as they might be, and his burning desire to associate with Shanghai's famous criminals, might be useful.

CHAPTER 22

THE PAST: 1934
PEKING

MATSUKO KNELT BEFORE HER SITTING father, both her knees firmly resting on the straw tatami mat spread out on the floor in front of his horseshoe-back chair. Her head was bowed, the tip of her chin lightly touching her chest. Her hands, locked in her father's hands, rested on top of his bent knees.

"You will not leave Peking, Matsuko-san. I forbid it."

"You cannot stop me, Father. I am no longer a child. I am going whether you approve or not. I hope you will accept that and will offer me your blessing."

She said this while continuing to bow her head. "If you do not bless me, I intend to go anyway. I will become a star on the stage in Shanghai."

Her father sighed. "I worry about you, Matsuko-san. But if you must go, my daughter, of course I give you my blessing."

He leaned forward and kissed the top of her head. "I must ask you, however, if the reason you have stated for going is the true reason?"

"It is, Father. I would never deceive you."

"*Hai!* I ask you, then, to make good use of your time among the enemy."

Matsuko shook her head, looking up now and staring into her father's eyes. She frowned.

"The Chinese are your enemy, Father, not mine. You act as if my beloved mother was not Chinese."

"I act as if we are now at war with these vermin. Your mother is no longer relevant to us in this capacity. The Emperor is relevant. Bushido is relevant. Nothing else, Matsuko. No one else."

Matsuko sighed. "You know I revere the Emperor, Father, and that I follow the Way of Bushido, but do not try to erase my memory of my mother from my life," she said, "not even in these present circumstances of conflict between our two cultures."

"It is not your mother I wish you to disregard and forget, my daughter. It is the others of her inferior race. All those Celestials who believe they are at the center of the universe, their Middle Kingdom, when all they really are, and soon will know that they are, are vassals of our *Mikado* — our Empero*r*."

Matsuko said nothing. She knew it was useless to argue with her father on this point.

"I have a task for you, Matsuko-san. While you are living in that deplorable city, I want you to serve the Emperor by listening and watching everything the enemy does, then report any important information back to me. Before you leave Peking, I will instruct you how to achieve this."

Matsuko again bowed her head, removed her hands from her father's, and straightened her back. She remained on her knees facing her father.

"*Hai! — Yes, Honorable Father!* Of course I will remember my duty to the Emperor and to the Code of Bushido when I am among the Celestials in Shanghai. I am, and always will be, your faithful and honorable daughter, a child of the Mikado, and a faithful follower of the Way of Bushido. You can rely on me."

CHAPTER 23

DAY ONE OF THE INVESTIGATION

I WENT DIRECTLY FROM BIG-EARED TU's home to Elder Brother's place of business.

———◆———

When I was sixteen years old, and Elder Brother was twenty-one, our parents, encouraged by the Lutheran missionaries who had converted my father from Taoism to Protestantism, sent us to San Francisco in America to study for four years at the mission college run by the Lutheran Church. Elder Brother and I entered the school at the same time and in the same grade even though we were five years apart in age. Fortunately, for most of our lives, our British mother had spoken English, as well as Mandarin Chinese, to us, and had insisted that we learn to read both languages. As a result, Elder Brother and I were able to pass our university courses and exams without difficulty.

School was free for us, including our food and a place to live, all paid for by the Lutheran Church. The only catch was that our parents had agreed that when Elder Brother and I graduated from college, we would become missionaries for the church.

When we returned to Shanghai after completing our studies, neither Elder Brother nor I honored that pledge. We didn't feel bad about this since we hadn't been the ones to make it in the first place, and likely, if asked to make it at the time, would not have agreed to do so. I cannot speak for Elder Brother with regard to this matter, but I would not have gone to America to attend college if I had known I would have to honor that pledge when I returned to Shanghai. I would have preferred ignorance to an education.

As I entered Sun-yu's nightclub, memories flooded back. It had been almost two years since I'd come here, and on that last occasion, as this time, I had come to ask Elder Brother for his help. I wondered if Sun-yu would resent my presence here today since I had stayed away so long. I'd probably resent that if I were him.

I intended to disclose to Sun-yu the nature of my investigation and to seek his assistance. Curiously, having done this already with Big-Eared Tu, I now felt few qualms about doing it again. That, I supposed, was the fruit of necessity.

Although Sun-yu is five years older than I am, much more than our birth dates separate us. We are fundamentally different people, as reflected in our differing approaches to conducting our lives.

I am a Confucian who believes in rules and order. I govern my life based on rules and order, although I do stray from time-to-time. Sun-yu, on the other hand, is a Taoist. He believes in permitting things to take their own course, without regard to man-made rules. These differences are fundamental to our respective ways of living day-to-day.

Sun-yu owns a prosperous nightclub on Avenue Edouard VII in the French Concession. The club is called the Heavenly Palace. He has used the club to fuel (but not yet to achieve) his ambition to become a notorious gangster — a *pai hsiag jen* — a member of one of Big-Eared Tu's Shanghai triads.

Sun-yu uses the club to cement and deepen his underworld connections, such as they are. To achieve this, he offers discounted drinks to the city's gangsters and free drinks to their female companions when they visit his club. So far, unfortunately for my brother, in spite of his desires and generous or foolish efforts with respect to his customer-gangsters, Sun-yu remains only a wannabe criminal, looking in from the outside, his broad, yellow nose pressed against crime's window.

When Sun-yu purchased the Heavenly Palace twelve years ago — it then was named the Pale Tea Club — he changed its name, upgraded its interior décor to western-style Art Deco, and eliminated several of the operating policies imposed on the club by its former owner, including the rule which had restricted the club's clientele to white-skin Round-Eyes only. Under Sun-yu's ownership, the only color the club recognizes is the color of gold, silver, and folding currency. In the Heavenly Palace, all cultures and races — white, Chinese, Jewish, Slavic, Colored, Russian, and even Dwarf Bandits, among others — are welcome if they can pay their way, cash for services, no chits, no monthly bill-collecting *shroffs* to visit your home or place of business. Cash only.

One of Elder Brother's first new practices when he assumed ownership of the club has proven to be very popular. Sun-yu brings in a different American jazz quartet or jazz band every two weeks, American jazz having been a favorite style of music in Shanghai since the late 1920s.

The club's other popular entertainment is taxi dancing — dancing with the club's hostesses for the price of a ticket per dance. Elder Brother operates this form of entertainment on the second floor of the club, once again ignoring Shanghai's customs by permitting both Chinese and White Russian women to act as taxi dancers and as flower-seller girls, all having access to the dance floor and to rooms to rent by the hour on the third floor of the club.

Although Elder Brother does not care about the various races or cultures of his taxi-dancing hostesses, he does very much care how attractive and how enticing his dancers look. All of Elder Brother's hostesses are tall, slim, and beautiful. All wear fashionable, tight-fitting dresses — called *chi-pao* — which cling to their bodies and are slit on the right side from their ankle-length hems up to the middle of their thighs. Sun-yu's taxi-dancing hostesses, as do hostesses in most of the other clubs, wear these seductive dresses while walking and dancing in very tall high-heels.

"Good afternoon, Elder Brother," I said, as I entered his office in the back of the club.

Sun-yu looked up and broke into a big smile. "*Heya!* —

Hello. What a nice surprise. Come in. Sit." He waved me into his cramped office.

We sat at a table, smoked Sun-yu's very strong *Hatamen*-brand cigarettes, and drank Tiger Wine, that foul-smelling drink made from tiger bones that have marinated in, and have disintegrated in, rice wine. We both have always felt ambivalent about this wine because of its foul odor, but often drank it together as we grew older so we could benefit from its long-term, aphrodisiacal properties as we aged and as nature otherwise took its toll on our maleness.

As I did with Big-Eared Tu, I proceeded to break all the rules Chief Inspector Chapman had set out for me to follow. I described, in complete detail, my conversation with the chief inspector, the crime I was investigating, the restrictions Chapman had imposed on me, my futile meeting with my informants, my meeting with Big-Eared Tu, and what little I had learned so far about the Yellow Swan.

"*Ayeeyah!* Seven days," Elder Brother said, "that does not give you much time before the saber drops. Will he really arrest you?"

I shrugged. "I don't know, but I must proceed as if he will. That's why I need your help."

"Of course." Sun-yu bowed his head briefly, then looked back into my eyes. "What can I do for you?"

"I need a full picture of the Yellow Swan. Where she came from before she arrived in Shanghai. Any criminal history she might have. Her family information. Why she came to Shanghai in the first place.

"You know what I mean. The usual. Anything you can learn about her, especially from before she arrived here, although anything else would be good, too.

"I have so little to go on, and so few sources now I can call upon for help, I need to know anything at all your connections can tell me. Right now, I am without resources or direction, and time is running out. The clock is ticking away."

Sun-yu nodded and refilled my glass. He lit another cigarette.

"One other thing," I said. "I need a plausible cover story why I'm asking questions about the Yellow Swan's death. Otherwise, people might wonder if I am investigating the crime."

"Any suggestions for a good story?" Sun-yu asked.

I shook my head. "None."

Elder Brother gazed across the room, then looked back at me and said, "How about saying you are writing a story about that woman for one of Shanghai's newspapers? I'm sure I can find someone who will give you an introduction to an editor, to someone who will tell that story if asked about you, if that's what you want."

I smiled. "That will be perfect. Please arrange for that as soon as possible."

"Consider it done, Younger Brother."

CHAPTER 24

THE PRESENT

AFTER SUN-JIN LEFT HIM, Tu thought about Sun-jin's request for help. Not everything the former inspector detective said was to be readily dismissed, he decided, although, for reasons of habit and prudence, he was not ready to openly join Sun-jin in his effort to solve the murder and to avoid an artificial political incident that might be manufactured by the local Dwarf Bandits and their looming military forces.

Big-Eared Tu had his servant summon Pock-Marked Huang to the Great Room.

"The former policeman, the one who solved the murders of the flower-seller girls, visited me today," Tu said. "He now works illegally as a private investigator."

"*Ayeeyah!* What concern is that of ours, Master Tu?"

Tu explained the nature of Sun-jin's visit.

"The ex-policemen was correct," Tu said. "An incident in the Settlement or in the French Concession will be bad for business. Possibly even worse if I do nothing to prevent it."

Huang nodded, patiently waiting to learn why Tu had summoned him to the Great Room, and why Tu was telling him about the former inspector detective's visit.

"I have not yet decided how to proceed," Tu said. "You will have the ex-policeman watched, day and night. Take any steps necessary to prevent him from provoking an incident with the Dwarf Bandits when he investigates the murder of the *low faan* woman."

"*Ayeeyah*," Huang said. "We will watch him day and night, as you wish, Master Tu."

"Pay close attention to the Dwarf Bandits. If they seem provoked by the former policeman, step in quickly to remove him from the situation."

Huang nodded. "That might mean we should step in to protect him or it could indicate we should step in to eliminate him."

Tu shrugged. "As you see fit," he said. "Keep me informed of his activity. It might be in our best interest at some point to assist him as he attempts to solve the murder. We can determine that when we need to."

CHAPTER 25

THE PRESENT

SMP INSPECTOR DETECTIVE MA WANG sat at his desk in SMP headquarters in the International Settlement. He studied the official Murder Book he'd put together.

The Murder Book, so far, remained thin. It contained the autopsy report for the Yellow Swan, the various lab reports regarding forensics at the crime scene, photos made of the dead woman, and other crime scene photos taken by the police photographer, the fingerprint report concerning the victim and the many other people who had visited the victim's changing room from time-to-time, and Ma's notes concerning his general observations, initial impressions at the crime scene, and interviews at the Tower Club. That was it so far.

Not much to go on, he thought.

The victim's fingerprints yielded no information about the Yellow Swan. Apparently she had kept her nose clean, although, as Ma laughed to himself when he thought about this, not clean enough, according to the coroner's report, which indicated she'd had a cocaine and opium habit that had damaged the linings of her nose and damaged her lungs.

The fingerprint report concerning the overall crime scene

was too full of information to be useful. There were too many prints from too many people who had been in and out of the changing room in the days or weeks preceding the homicide to be able to eliminate suspects. As soon as any of the prints were identified, Ma decided, he would send out some junior, sub-inspector detective to interview each of the ID'd subjects, rather than waste his time doing that himself.

As he often did these days in homicide cases, Ma called forth his ten years' experience to reach a preliminary conclusion about the homicide he was investigating. In this instance, based on little evidence, some speculation, and his well-grounded intuition — and with the imperative to quickly wrap-up his investigation or suffer the wrath of Chief Inspector Chapman, who was pushing him to obtain a fast result — Ma concluded, based on the nature and extent of the Yellow Swan's neck injuries, that the murder of the Yellow Swan had been a crime of passion. The motive, however, so-far remained a mystery to him.

CHAPTER 26

THE PAST: 1934

PEKING

THE NIGHT BEFORE MATSUKO WAS to board the Iron Rooster passenger train that would carry her from Peking to Shanghai, Kanji visited her in her home. Matsuko's father was not there.

"I'll hear no more of that, Kanji-san," Matsuko said, crossing her arms over her chest. "We have argued enough about this. Arrangements have been made. I am going."

Kanji stiffened. "I love you. We belong here together."

Matsuko tapped her foot, but said nothing. Her eyes narrowed into a severe frown.

"Shanghai is abominable, Matsuko-san. You do not belong in such a city. It is corrupt. If you go, that whore of a city will corrupt you, too. It destroys everyone."

"I have made up my mind. You cannot change it. You must stop trying to do so or you must leave now."

"That city will ruin you."

Matsuko laughed and shook her head. She walked over to

Kanji, took his chin in her fingers, then leaned in and lightly kissed him on his lips.

"You are acting like a fool, Kanji-san, although a loving fool." She smiled. "You cannot frighten me into staying here. I am not a child. I will take care to protect myself. I am not corruptible. I am Bushido."

Kanji sighed. "The fact that you believe such a foolish thought shows how naïve and corruptible you are."

Matsuko laughed. "Actually, I do not believe that," she said, "but I thought you might if I said it. You know me well-enough to know this. I also believe my Bushido creed might not be enough to protect me there, but I have no choice but to go."

"No choice? What is it you are saying? You can change your mind. The elderly Round-Eyes cannot force you to go to Shanghai if you decline."

Matsuko pouted briefly, looked up at Kanji with sad eyes, then said, "I must go, Kanji-san, although I do not want to. I have no desire to leave you or to leave Peking. I am happy here with my life.

"My father has insisted I go. Moving to Shanghai was his idea, his way of assuring I can serve the Emperor as a spy against the Celestials." She paused and took a deep breath. "Yet I am afraid to go, Kanji-san." She slowly lowered her eyes.

"*Hai!*" Kanji squared his shoulders, standing taller. He took Matsuko's hands in his. "I will speak to your father. I will change his mind for you. It is settled. You will not go."

"No, no, no, Kanji-san, do not do that." She shook her head. "Do not even think about doing that." She kissed his forehead. "That would greatly upset my father.

"He is so proud of his idea to send me to Shanghai to serve the Emperor." She paused briefly, looked directly into Kanji's eyes, then said, speaking softly, "You must leave now. I have matters to arrange before I travel."

"Matsuko," Kanji said, as he took both her hands in his. "Remember your Code of Bushido. Do not fraternize with the Celestials while in Shanghai. They are inferior beings who will seek to subvert your values and to foment disloyalty to the Emperor. Never forget, they are the enemy."

"Of course, Kanji-san." Her face darkened. "But you insult me. Why do you believe you must remind me of the obvious. I know my duty. I am fully aware of my role in society." She stepped back, just away from his reach.

"Do not patronize me, Kanji-san. I am not a child. I will develop spy sources other than the Celestials to find out information that will assist father and the Emperor."

Kanji took a deep breath, then slowly sighed. "Please do not go, Matsuko-san. I foresee bad things happening to you if you go."

Matsuko shook her head. "You must leave now, Kanji."

"Please, Matsuko-san."

"I told you. I have no choice. I do want to stay in Peking with you, Kanji-san, but I must obey my father and follow his wish that I move to Shanghai. I am so sad."

CHAPTER 27

DAY ONE OF THE INVESTIGATION

LEFT ELDER BROTHER AND, AS I rode the electric trolley back to the Settlement, considered what to do next. I knew I couldn't risk returning to the Cathay Hotel and possibly running into Harue again, so I decided, for the time being, to regroup and do some additional research concerning the Yellow Swan. I believed that if I could learn more about this young woman, I would be more likely to discover who might have wanted her dead.

I departed the trolley at The Bund, and again walked over to Fusan Avenue to the Shanghai Public Library. As I approached the large, iron doors of the building, I touched one of the two statues of bronze lions that flanked the entrance. Doing this, as everyone knows, is good *joss*. I again found my way to the room having old copies of newspapers.

I researched the past issues of various out-of-town newspapers. This was tedious because I did not know which out of-town newspapers might be relevant since I did not yet know where the Yellow Swan had lived before she appeared in Shanghai.

I first paged through back issues of the *Tientsin Daily News,* then through the *China Press,* the Canton *China Times*, the Nanking *Lotus Star,* and the Peking *Double Lotus Times*. I even searched through back-issues of the English-language Dwarf Bandit newspaper published in Shanghai — the *Honshu Cherry Blossom Press*. All the newspapers were long on speculation and gossip, but short on facts concerning the Yellow Swan, especially about her mysterious past.

I spent three hours in the newspaper morgue. The time was not very productive. I was barely able to put together a sketchy, composite portrait of the young woman, basing my picture of her on various accounts offered by a few of the newspapers I paged through.

The portrait I drew from the newspapers did not add much to what the chief inspector had told me, and was not very helpful. It amounted to this: The Yellow Swan was somewhere around twenty-four to twenty-seven years old when she died. She seemed to be unmarried. Her singing voice, while beautiful, reflected a lack of formal training. And, obviously, she was Asian, possibly Chinese, but likely Japanese, too, as the chief inspector had said.

The Yellow Swan clearly had had a mysterious past she'd decided to hide when she came to Shanghai. Else why was she so private?

The question was not only what was she hiding about her past, but why was she hiding it? *And,* I wondered, *had her mysterious past finally caught up with her?*

I thought about this, and realized that the Yellow Swan's actions really weren't much different, if different at all, from the many immigrants who have come to Shanghai over the years to reinvent themselves — immigrants who are both Oriental and Occidental.

The unwritten code of the city is that no one delves too closely, if at all, into the past lives of people who now live in Shanghai. We take such people at their current face value, however they present themselves to us. That is one of the beautiful things about Shanghai, but is both its strength and its weakness.

Under other circumstances, if someone else had been involved, I would have reflexively abided by this code and would not have taken on the case forced on me by Chief Inspector Chapman.

The problem with the Yellow Swan, however, was that there wasn't even any so-called "face value to take her a" for the present, and I didn't have the luxury of not examining her past to find out who she really had been before she arrived here. I was running out of time. Besides, she was dead, so, I assumed, she wouldn't care if I snooped.

CHAPTER 28

THE PRESENT

JMP Inspector Detective Harue proceeded to follow the order given to him by the Kwantung officer. He would find an excuse to use the young woman's death to manufacture a political and military incident. As his first step in this direction, Harue strode into the lobby of the Cathay Hotel and glanced around. He planned to visit the scene of the crime.

As he started to walk over to the registration desk to inquire about the room number of the Yellow Swan's changing room, he glanced toward the bank of closed lift doors directly ahead of him. As he stared, the left door opened and one passenger stepped out of the lift.

That man looks familiar, Harue thought.

Their eyes met briefly. Then the man abruptly looked away, turned around, and stepped back into the lift.

Harue watched the man's arm stab at the lift's button panel until the door closed. Harue's eyes followed the floor-indicator above the door until the arrow indicated that the lift had reached the second floor and stopped.

Ah! He suddenly remembered who he'd just glimpsed. *That*

was former SMP Inspector Detective Sun-jin. What's he doing here? He has no business with this investigation. He's no longer a Special Branch policeman.

Harue walked over to the registration desk. Using halting English, he said, "Where was the changing room of the woman known as the Yellow Swan?"

"Ninth Floor," the clerk behind the desk answered.

"*Hai.* Nine?"

"Yes, sir."

"Not two?"

"No, sir. As I said, nine."

Interesting. Why then did the former SMP policeman stop the lift on the second floor after he saw me?

CHAPTER 29

DAY ONE OF THE INVESTIGATION

ELDER BROTHER CALLED AND SUGGESTED we meet again. He said he had some information I might find useful.

We settled into his office, again smoked cigarettes, and finished the bottle of Tiger Wine we'd started before.

"My triad colleagues have gathered some information concerning the Yellow Swan," Sun-yu said, "but I don't know how useful it will be to your investigation."

"It will be better to know whatever you might tell me," I said, "than not to know." I sat back, sipped my Tiger Wine, and waited.

"Her mother was Chinese," Sun-yu said. "Her father a Dwarf Bandit. Her true name was Matsuko Akasuki."

"That's not Chinese," I said. "I would have assumed she would have been named after her mother's family as tradition requires, not according to her father's culture."

"Her father is a minor functionary in the Dwarf Bandit's Consulate in Peking. He has a reputation for being virulently anti-Chinese, ever since his Chinese wife mysteriously died years ago."

"The Yellow Swan was raised in Peking," Elder Brother

said, "and recruited to Shanghai by Victor Sassoon for his nightclub."

"How does that tie-in with her death?" I asked.

"I don't know. I am not interpreting the facts I gathered for you. I am merely reporting them. It will be up to you to determine which facts help your investigation and which do not."

"Of course," I said. "I'm sorry." I drew heavily on my cigarette.

"There's a rumor the Yellow Swan was an advocate of the Code of Bushido, and, at her father's request, was spying for the Kwantung army in Shanghai against our KMT military.

Now, that's something, I thought.

"Of course," Sun-yu said, "there also is a rumor that she was spying for Generalissimo Chiang's KMT army against the Dwarf Bandits, out of loyalty to her deceased mother, and that the Kwantung killed her to put a stop to that."

I shook my head. This was not helping me.

"I could not find out if she was a spy, Younger Brother, or, if she *was* a spy, for which side. Perhaps she was spying for each side against the other." He shrugged his shoulders and took a sip of his wine.

"I do know," he said, "that she kept personal relations with both Chinese and Dwarf Bandit men and women."

"Was she a flower-seller girl?" I said.

"Occasionally. The rumor is that she worked the Flowery Kingdom as a means of gaining military and political information." He paused to take a puff of his cigarette. "That is all I have learned."

I stood up. "Thank you, Elder Brother. As I said before,

every little piece of information, however murky it might initially seem, helps fill-in the picture I am trying to build."

"One other thing," Sun-yu said, as he put his hand lightly on my shoulder to restrain me. "I still am working on putting together your cover story. I expect soon to know the name of an editor or reporter who will consider buying your story about the Yellow Swan when you have written it."

CHAPTER 30

DAY ONE OF THE INVESTIGATION

A S THE FIRST DAY OF my investigation neared its end, Chief Inspector Chapman and I met again at the Willow Pattern Tea House.

"Making progress, Old Boy?" Chapman said.

I shrugged. "Some, but it's too early to know if it's meaningful progress. I need resources I don't have and cannot call upon. But you already know that."

Chapman said nothing. He briefly raised one eyebrow. Reminding him of the corner he'd boxed me into clearly annoyed him.

"I've confirmed what you told me — that the Yellow Swan's heritage was both Chinese and Dwarf Bandit, and that after her mother died when the Yellow Swan was seven years old, she was raised by her father as if she was a full-blooded Dwarf Bandit." I told Chapman her true name.

"Apparently, her father, a minor diplomat in Peking all the years of her life, infused the Yellow Swan with the Way of Bushido."

"That might mean something," Chapman said.

"It might mean she was in Shanghai as an agent for the

Dwarf Bandits, and that her spying got her killed by we Chinese."

"That's a possibility, of course, but without some confirmation, it's pretty far-fetched that she was a Jap spy since she had a Chinese mother," Chapman said. "Do you have any evidence to back up your suggestion?"

"I've also learned she was equally friendly with Chinese men and women and with Dwarf Bandit men and women," I said. "That could have angered anyone in the current political climate."

Chapman nodded. "It's possible she wasn't murdered because of her politics, but was killed because she was too friendly with the wrong people. Problem is, which people? Japs or Chinese? And, if one or the other, murdered by which one?"

Chapman tapped ashes from his pipe into his empty tea cup.

"Well, Old Boy," he continued, "time is ticking away. Only six days left to resolve this, unless the Japs act before then. You better promptly wrap this up before that happens. Don't force me to arrest you."

When I left the chief inspector, I decided that, notwithstanding the chance I might run into JMP Inspector Detective Harue again, I had no choice but to return to the scene of the crime. I climbed aboard a rickshaw, gave directions to the pulling coolie, and settled back for a rapid, bone-jarring ride to the hotel.

I wanted to look around the Cathay again to try to find some witnesses — hotel employees — who could tell me more about the young woman, or employees who had seen something unusual, the day or night she was killed. And I still needed more basic information concerning the Yellow Swan.

I looked around as I entered the lobby, hoping I would not see Harue. I did not. I decided I would have to take the chance of running into him on the ninth floor if I wanted to talk to employees of the Tower Club. It was late enough in the day that some employees might now be there setting up for this evening.

I was heading for the lift when someone grabbed my shoulder. I abruptly stopped and spun around, ready to force the hand off me. I found myself standing face-to-face with JSP Inspector Detective Akio Harue.

CHAPTER 31

THE PRESENT

SMP Special Branch Inspector Detective Ma Wang returned to the scene of the crime. When he stepped off the lift to head to the Yellow Swan's changing room, he could see that the door to the room down the hallway was open.

He fumed. *I never gave anyone permission to enter the crime scene.*

He slowly pushed open the door, peered inside, then cautiously stepped in.

"*Ayeeyah!* What are you doing in here?" Ma said to the man standing across the room, his back to the door, looking out the window.

The young man, startled, jumped and turned to face Ma.

Ma noted that the young man was dressed in a pageboy's uniform. *An employee of the hotel, no doubt,* he thought.

"I said, what are you doing here? This is a crime scene. It's off limits."

The young man blushed. "I didn't mean no harm, Mate. I was just lookin' around, remembering the Yellow Swan."

"You have no business here," Ma said. "I should report you

to your boss and have you removed from your job. What's your name?"

The pageboy told him. "I'm not the only one's been here. Not by a long shot, you know."

That gave Ma pause. He inhaled deeply. "*Maskee? — What are you talking about?* This room is officially off limits. Who else came in here?"

"A fan. An admirer of the Yellow Swan. He didn't do no harm. He just looked around, then left."

I need to find that person. He could be involved in the homicide, returning to the scene of his crime.

"What was his name? Do you know where I can find him, this admirer of the victim?"

The pageboy shook his head. "No idea. Didn't ask his name and haven't seen him since."

Ma ordered the pageboy to stay out of the Yellow Swan's changing room.

"Now, you listen to me if you know what's good for you," Ma said. "From now on, you don't talk to anyone about this case. That means no one except me. No one else, even if he's a cop. Understand?

"That goes for everyone who works here, too. You spread the word if you know what's good for you, now that I have your name. No one talks to anyone but me."

"Yes, sir."

Ma made sure the pageboy left the area, then he headed back to headquarters to report the anomalous visit of one of the Yellow Swan's fans to Chief Inspector Chapman. As he left the hotel, he did not notice Inspector Detective Harue and Sun-jin moving away from the entrance, heading toward the side of the lobby.

CHAPTER 32

THE PAST: 1934

KANJI HAD NEVER BEFORE BEEN to Shanghai, but he did not find it difficult to locate his Yakuza brother. Word of his arrival in Shanghai had preceded him from Peking.

"Then you will keep watch over Matsuko Akasuki, as I wish," he said, "and will report back to me?"

"I will be honored, my brother. You have my vow. I will observe the young woman's daily life. My reports to you will be thorough."

"No matter how long this might continue?" Kanji said.

"I will watch her, brother, for however long I must. Even for years if that is what you want."

CHAPTER 33

DAY ONE OF THE INVESTIGATION

HARUE DID NOT RELEASE HIS hand from my shoulder when we faced one another.

"Good afternoon, ex-Inspector Detective," Harue said. He tightened his grip on my shoulder as if to prevent me from running away.

"This is the second time today I have seen you in this hotel lobby. Why are you here?"

"Personal business," I said. "Keep your hand off my shoulder." I reached up and deliberately removed his hand.

"Come with me," Harue said. "I have questions for you." He pointed across the lobby to a secluded spot away from the hotel's front entrance, the lifts, and the registration desk.

He rested one hand on the butt of his pistol as he said this to me. His tone of voice and his bearing did not suggest I had any option but to follow him across the lobby, so I did.

———◆———

"You are interfering with an official police investigation," he said. "I can arrest you for that."

"*Ayeeyah!* I'm doing no such thing. I told you, I'm here on personal business. You have no right accusing me of anything."

"I don't believe you."

"*Dui bu qi — Too bad.* I don't really care what you believe. Besides," I said, "you are JMP, not SMP. What are *you* doing in this part of the Settlement? You don't have jurisdiction outside Hongkew."

"You are wrong. The murder of the young Japanese citizen who sang in this hotel is no longer a matter for just the SMP to investigate.

"The murder is more than a mere crime. The murder of the Yellow Swan is also a political and military matter. The investigation is now in the hands of the Kwantung and the Japanese government, not just the police."

He sneered. "I am the authorized representative of the Kwantung army and of the Japanese government, with full jurisdiction to investigate and resolve this murder everywhere the evidence might take me." He looked hard at me and squared his shoulders. His palm rested on this saber.

I didn't know if what he said was true or not, or if the fact that he'd said it in itself conferred the authority in the Settlement he claimed to have. I did know that if I weren't careful, Harue could become a difficult obstacle for me to overcome as I raced the clock to solve this crime.

"I don't believe you have such authority, Harue," I said. I wanted to see how certain he would be if I challenged him.

"You will stay away from this hotel and away from my investigation," he said, "or I will arrest you. Do you understand?"

I left the hotel and, not seeing a taxi, rode a rickshaw home. As

I approached my apartment building, Bik came running over to me. She jumped up and down and wagged her tail, apparently as happy to see me as I was to see her. I took her inside, fed her, refilled her water bowl, and then put her outside again to run around while I settled down to work.

I considered my situation. I had six days left, at most, to solve the murder or be arrested by Chief Inspector Chapman. Meanwhile, I had to avoid being arrested by Harue for trying to solve the murder and, as he saw it, interfering with his police, political, and military investigation.

I sat down in my kitchen, poured myself a glass of *Baijiu* — Chinese vodka — and plotted my course of action for tomorrow, Day Two of my investigation.

PART TWO

CHAPTER 34

DAY TWO OF THE INVESTIGATION

ELDER BROTHER'S TRIAD CONTACTS CAME through with some other useful information for me. I would never again think ill of Sun-yu merely because he wanted to be an acknowledged member of Shanghai's gangster community. This was the second time in my adult life I'd come to him for help, and both times his underworld contacts helped me.

One of the White Peony Beneficent Society's members told Elder Brother that he had often seen the Yellow Swan at after-hours clubs late in the evenings and early mornings, after she finished performing at the Tower Club.

One of Sun-yu's triad contacts also told him where the Yellow Swan lived before she died. He knew this, he said, because, in his occasional capacity as a taxicab driver, he'd frequently driven her home in the early-morning hours after the clubs closed, often when the Yellow Swan had been in no condition to navigate her way to a taxi or make it home on her own. He said he carried her up to her apartment several times and put her on her sofa to sleep before he left.

"She lived," Elder Brother said, in a luxury suite at the Broadway Mansions Apartments in Hongkew."

I fed Bik, put her water bowl outside our apartment building so she could drink during the day before I returned home, and let her outside for the day. Then I headed to Hongkew to visit the Broadway Mansions Apartments.

Hongkew consists of that part of the International Settlement situated north of Soochow Creek. It used to be known as the American Settlement until the Americans and British combined their treaty Concessions into one territory, and renamed that territory the International Settlement.

Hongkew can best be reached by crossing over the Garden Bridge or one of the other nearby bridges that span Soochow Creek at Honan and Szechuen Roads. I chose to go over the Garden Bridge.

Until it was deserted by the Americans, Hongkew was considered a desirable place to live and work. When the Americans left, however, their places were taken by swarms of poor Dwarf Bandits who were imported from the mother country to perform coolie-type and flower-seller girls' work for the more affluent Dwarf Bandits who lived there.

With the opening in 1934 of the luxurious Broadway Mansions, however, and the continuing operation of the extraordinary, city-block-wide, multi-story Hongkew Market — which serves the entire city — the prevailing rumor throughout Shanghai was that Hongkew might one day again be a desirable place to live and work. I doubt this, however, since it continues to become more and more crowded as more Dwarf Bandits flood in.

I walked through the Public Gardens, heading for the bridge, careful to avoid any roving SMP constables who, if they noticed me, would ask for my identification and for my reason for being in the park, where, by law, we Chinese and dogs usually are not permitted. I took this route because it was the shortest way to reach Matsuko's apartment building when coming from the Settlement.

I could see the Broadway Mansions as I left the Public Gardens and walked across the Garden Bridge. As I approached the front entrance of the building, I thought about what I'd read about the Broadway Mansions in the three years since it opened for business. I have never been inside the building, although I have often seen it from both sides of the river.

When the Broadway Mansions opened for business, its sixteen stories made it the tallest building in Shanghai. The building's south-facing façade, correctly situated to satisfy the requirements of *Feng Shui*, has a full, panoramic view of the Bund and of the Bund's high-rise buildings across the water.

Notwithstanding its name, the building operates as if it were a luxury hotel rather than as an apartment house. Its suites come fully furnished with everything a long-term resident could want, including maid service and food and beverage services. The apartments are fitted-out with electric lights, palatial bathrooms, steam heating, and glass in the windows instead of translucent paper.

The ninety-nine apartments were designed as perfect bachelor pads, to use a term currently in vogue, for young men and women. Each apartment has a sitting room with a fold-up-into-the-wall bed, a luxuriously appointed bathroom with indoor plumbing, a small kitchen with the most modern gas appliances, and a separate changing room. All apartments are serviced by the building's modern heating and air conditioning systems.

The fifth floor of the structure is taken up by a dining room seating 218 people. The dining room is decorated in shades of tan and gold, with beige table cloths. The theme is Art Deco. The Foreign Correspondents' Club occupies the top floor of the building.

The back of the building, which I hadn't paid much attention to over the years, and have only seen when I've left Hongkew on other occasions and have headed for the Garden Bridge, consists of a four-story structure that butts-out from the main building. It is used as a car park, having spaces for 163 cars that can be driven up and down ramps, to and from each car's lock-up space. A modern lift carries drivers up and down the car park.

The building and land are owned and operated by the Shanghai Land and Investment Company, Victor Sassoon's real estate firm.

As I approached the building's entrance and looked at the tall Sikh who, dressed in an orange head-dress and white tunic, stood sentry outside the front doors, I wondered how a young woman, who ostensibly earned her living as a nightclub chanteuse and occasional flower-seller girl, could afford to live in a luxurious place like this.

As I neared the doors, the Sikh said, "May I be of assistance to you, sir?" He bowed slightly from his waist, but never took his eyes off me. As he asked this, he moved to block the doorway, not at all being subtle about it.

I looked up at him. He was about three-quarters of a meter taller than I am, younger, much broader, and, to all appearances, much more fit than I am even though I practice *Shaolin* every morning.

"*Shi — Yes,* I said. "I'm a private investigator. I'm here to talk to anyone who knows anything about Matsuko Akasuki, the Yellow Swan, a former, recent resident of this building. She's now dead, unfortunately, in case you didn't know."

"Sorry, honorable sir," he said, "but we do not permit solicitations here. The residents require that we respect their privacy."

"That's noble," I said, "except Miss Akasuki in no longer a resident and has no expectations. As I said, she's dead. Murdered. She no longer expects you to safeguard her privacy."

The Sikh didn't budge from his place in front of the doors. He crossed his arms over his capacious chest and continued to block my way. He now looked down at me, it seemed, with contempt in his eyes.

"Good day, sir."

I nodded at the man, then turned and walked back down the path, away from the front doors. There was no point in wasting time trying to convince him to let me enter the building. He had a job to do, though he misconceived its purpose, and would likely not budge from his perception of what his job was and how he should perform it. I would never be able to convince him that dead people do not care about their privacy.

I headed home. I would go forward this afternoon to learn more about the Yellow Swan's after-hours' night life now that I knew from Elder Brother that she'd had one.

CHAPTER 35

THE PRESENT

Inspector Detective Ma Wang watched Chief Inspector Chapman as the chief stepped through the ritual he always followed to fill and light his pipe.

He waited until Chapman exhaled a cloud of smoke and then looked up. He again had the chief inspector's full attention. Ma continued his report.

"So, Chief Inspector, that's my account of the investigation so far, except for one odd matter you should know about."

"What's that, Old Boy?"

"When I interviewed one of the hotel's employees — a pageboy — he said someone else had come around the crime scene asking questions. This person also looked into the victim's changing room." He paused briefly. "Is someone else assigned to this case, sir, besides me?"

Chapman shook his head. "It's your case, Inspector Detective."

"But, sir, someone definitely was there asking investigative-type questions. Perhaps someone masquerading as an inspector detective for some reason we don't know about. I'll find out who and look him up."

"Don't bother," Chapman said. "You cannot afford the time. You need to solve the crime before the Japs take advantage of the murder to declare an international incident. I've already told you that."

"But—"

"Probably was a reporter trying to get a story about the Yellow Swan. Don't put any time into it, Inspector Detective. That's an order."

Ma frowned. "Yes, sir." He shook his head slightly. "There's one more thing, sir, based on what the pageboy told me."

"Go on."

"I instructed him — and I told the pageboy to tell all the other employees at the hotel — not to speak to anyone except me about the Yellow Swan, the crime or the investigation since I'm officially handling the case.

"I also ordered him to keep everyone, including himself, out of the Yellow Swan's changing room even though it's been emptied out. You never know what might turn up later in my investigation that will require me to go back there for another look."

"Smart moves, Old Boy," Chapman said, "That should discourage that reporter."

CHAPTER 36

THE PAST: 1934

K ANJI RELUCTANTLY MADE ANOTHER VISIT to Shanghai, his first since he originally arranged to have his Yakuza brother watch Matsuko for him. He was not happy to be there. He looked forward to leaving the city later that afternoon and returning to Peking. If all went as he planned, he would leave Shanghai with Matsuko in tow.

It had taken all his persuasive powers, including veiled threats of harm by him or his Yakuza brothers, to convince the Sikh sentry at the building's entrance to allow him to enter the lobby and use the telephone located there to call Matsuko's apartment. It then had taken all his persuasive powers to convince Matsuko to allow him to visit her upstairs. The telephone call he placed to her from the lobby had been strained.

"What do you mean you're in the lobby of my building?" Matsuko said. "Why aren't you in Peking?"

"I am here to talk to you."

"How did you find me? How did you know where I live? No one knows that."

"My Yakuza brother informed me after I asked him to find this out for me."

"Are you having me watched? Is that it?" Matsuko said. "Are you now hunting me like some kind of prey?"

Kanji had never been in a luxury apartment before. He was overwhelmed with the opulence and the spacial waste he observed when Matsuko admitted him into her home.

Kanji glanced past Matsuko as he removed his sandals, and then stepped into the foyer.

"Show me around this living quarters," he said.

Nothing he saw would have suggested to him that the apartment was occupied by a Japanese national, let alone one who professed to be loyal to the homeland, to the Way of Bushido, and to the Emperor. Instead, everything in Matsuko's home — the unmade bed hanging open from a wall, rather than the traditional tatami mat; the stand-alone A-frame wardrobe, with its open door, containing her Celestial and some western-style clothes; the three Chinese horseback chairs in the living room; and, the Art Deco sofa — all suggested to him that Matsuko had renounced her heritage and had succumbed to the effete world of the Celestials.

"You must come home to Peking with me at once," he said to her, "and give up this decadent life." He swept his arm widely to corral the entire living room.

"I am home. Shanghai is now my home."

"Peking is your home."

Matsuko's face darkened. She felt her neck grow warm. "What makes you think I do not live a righteous life in Shanghai? Are you spying on me?"

"You must return to the Way of Bushido," Kanji said.

"I live a righteous life here. I have no need or desire to return to Peking."

"Do you pillow with the enemy? Have you become a concubine of a Celestial Being?"

"Of course not," Matsuko said. "There are limits to what I would do. I know my place in Bushido."

"Return with me today before it is too late," Kanji said.

Matsuko shook her head and laughed a joyless laugh. "Stop bothering me, Kanji-san. Go home. Return to Peking. My life is here. I have no need for you to lecture me or have me watched for you."

Kanji felt his hand reflexively grip his throwing star that was lodged in his belt. He yanked his hand back as if his fingers had been scalded.

"Come with me, Matsuko-san. We will leave together now."

She shook her head and stepped back, far away from Kanji.

"You are an old fool, Kanji-san. Don't you see that my life now is here in Shanghai, not in Peking? I have no need for Peking or for the life it offers me. That life no longer fits me. Go now. I do not want you here," she said.

"Matsuko—"

"I am not Matsuko. Not any longer. I am the Yellow Swan. If I should ever happen to see you again, I insist you refer to me as the Yellow Swan. Matsuko's life is behind me, left permanently in Peking. Now go," she said.

She walked into the foyer and opened the door leading to the hallway, her hand resting on the doorknob as she waited for Kanji to pass by.

CHAPTER 37

THE RECENT PAST: 1936

Bik awoke Mei-hua and me by hopping up onto my bed, jumping around, then licking our faces. The sun was not yet up.

Mei-hua sat up, rubbed her eyes, then ran her hand through Bik's fur, briskly stroking Bik's back.

"That's a good girl," Mei-hua said. "Does this feel nice for you?" Mei-hua laughed, as I squinted, only partly awake, at them.

"*Ayeeyah!* You can't wait 'til we're awake and up so you can kiss us, can you, you devil-dog?" Mei-hua said.

Bik jumped around on our bed wagging her tail.

I smiled at my two girls.

———— ❀ ————

Mei-hua and I sat at the bare wooden table in my kitchen. Bik laid on the floor under the table. Mei-hua and I drank coffee and shared a large piece of bread left over from dinner the night before.

Because I did not want to admit to myself that what Mei-hua was saying to me was potentially a problem for us, I only partially paid attention. I was having trouble following what she was telling me, therefore.

"I don't understand. You say your father wants you to drop me from your life because I used to be a cop? That doesn't make sense. Haven't you told him my history, that I have no loyalty to the SMP?"

"Don't worry, Sun-jin." Mei-hua patted my hand. "I'm not going to give you up just because he wants me to."

"Why should he care, unless he's a criminal?" I said.

Mei-hua's eyebrows shot up. She laughed. "Of course he's a criminal. He's a career officer in the KMT, after all. All Chiang's officers — like the generalissimo himself — are decadent and corrupt, are tools of rampant capitalism." She laughed at her comment and Sun-jin's apparent naiveté.

I smiled, but wasn't sure if Mei-hua believed that or had just said it for my benefit.

"He also wants me to publicly renounce my former CCP membership and activities. He says my failure to do so continues to hurt his chances for promotion to general.

"What do you want to do?" I said.

"Not that," she said. "Not either thing. Don't worry, Sun-jin. I'm not letting you out of my life just because my father insists I do so. I make my own decisions. No one does that for me."

CHAPTER 38

DAY TWO OF THE INVESTIGATION

SINCE I'D HAD NO SUCCESS gaining access to the Broadway Mansions Apartments so I could question the Yellow Swan's neighbors and the building's employees, I decided to follow-up Elder Brother's other lead. I would visit the after-hours night clubs the Yellow Swan was known to frequent after the Tower Club closed at 3:00 a.m. Elder Brother had said that one club was called the Majestic Café; the other was known as the Del Monte Cabaret.

I went first to the Majestic Café, located in the Settlement at 254 Nanking Road, across the street from the site of the old race course. This club was known for catering to Hongkew's Dwarf Bandit population, who crossed the Whangpoo and came into the Round-Eyes' part of the Settlement for entertainment. Its ads claimed to have 100 charming and beautiful dance hostesses available every night.

The club's management discouraged Chinese and Round-Eyes from using its facilities as customers (but not as coolie-employees), although, under the terms of its after-hours operating license, it could not block those races from participating in club activities if someone insisted they be permitted to do so. Few Chinese or Round-Eyes ever so insisted.

Unlike most clubs in the Settlement, the Majestic Café was permitted to remain open after 3:00 a.m. because it had been doing so for at least fifty years before the Municipal Council passed the recent law prohibiting such late hours for clubs and cabarets. The notorious Round-Eyes writer named Emily Hahn — Mickey Hahn, as the Missouri-born writer was known here in the city — had even made-up and published a catchy phrase for such exceptions to the new closing-time law. She called these exceptions *grand-fathered clubs* because the right for these businesses to stay open had existed for half a century before the new law took effect, and would only apply to such old establishments.

It was 4:00 p.m. when I arrived at the Majestic. The entrance door was locked. A sign indicated the club would not open for business until 10:00 p.m. that evening. I didn't see any point in coming around asking questions in the evening when the club was open for business. No one working at night would want me to take up their time.

Based on what I knew about such clubs — all clubs, in fact — nothing would happen there until around midnight. Before that, during the afternoon and early evening, the club would be a place for flower-seller girls to meet and hang-out with their pimps, and a place for men to bring women they shouldn't be seen with.

I knocked hard on the front door, giving my strokes the authority I used when I was a Special Branch inspector detective.

After half a minute, and repeated knocking by me, the door opened a crack. I could see an elderly Chinese coolie-woman — likely a cleaning coolie — staring out at me.

"Ah, Auntie," I said, using the term we Chinese politely use when addressing an elderly woman we do not know, "I am here to speak to someone in authority about one of the club's patrons."

She responded to me with cold silence.

I realized I had reflexively spoken in Mandarin, as I typically do when talking with someone educated. I immediately switched to the common dialect of the streets I'd been raised to speak, called *Hu* in Shanghainese. The woman understood me this time.

"*Ayeeyah!*" she said. She looked directly at me, leaned her head back slightly, elevating her chin, and rolled her eyes back into her head so as to show only their whites. She was giving me what we Chinese refer to as *Giving White Eyes,* a gesture that indicates contempt for the other person.

"You wait here," she finally said, when she'd finished her expression of distain. "Boss man not here. Round-Eyes man who writes numbers here. I get him." She closed the door, leaving me standing on the porch.

Less than a minute later, an Occidental man, who identified himself as the club's bookkeeper, came out to meet me. We walked into the club's entertaining room on the way to his office.

The club was sweltering as we crossed the floor. I

commented on this as we walked. "Is it always this hot? How do the customer-dancers stand it?"

"It's not this bad when we're open," the bookkeeper said. "Our ceiling fans run while we're open. They are powered by coolies working in shifts to keep them going."

"That really helps?" I asked. "Even with people dancing and sweating?"

"We place a dozen large blocks of ice in the middle of the dance floor," he said. "This cools off the dancers. Our coolies use mops between dances to clear the water off the floor."

I rolled my eyes, but said nothing.

As we walked across the entertaining room, heading, I assumed, to his office, I looked around. The room consisted of a large area with the dance floor in the center and a short wooden bar along one wall. There were twenty or so small tables scattered around the perimeter of the dance floor, each with four rickety-looking wooden chairs surrounding them.

Some fresh paint on the walls, I thought, *and perhaps table linens, the lights dimmed at night, and bustling waiters bringing cocaine, opium, and alcohol, would make this place habitable later in the evening.*

Even at this hour, with no patrons present and smoking, the air was thick with the smell of stale cigarette smoke and the bitter-sweet scent of burned drugs.

I looked at the shelves behind the bar as we walked past. They were stocked with ordinary whiskey, some inexpensive wines I recognized and occasionally drank, several off-brands of Saki, and some low-grade brandy. Nothing special or expensive there. Or, I should say, since the drinks likely were expensive to purchase, nothing of high quality I could see that would justify their likely high cost to drink.

According to several signs posted on the walls, this club, just like Elder Brother's club, was an establishment that required cash only. No chits. No *shroffs* — *bill collectors* — to visit the club's patrons once each month at their homes or places of work to collect their outstanding club chits. Unlike most of Shanghai, where reputable entertainment clubs put everything on the customer's tab, not ever accepting cash payment at the club, service at the Majestic Café, as the flower-seller girls who worked this neighborhood would say, was strictly cash only.

The bookkeeper and I walked into a small room he seemed to be using as an office.

"A private investigator, are you?" he said, as soon as we settled into our seats.

I nodded. "I'm investigating the murder of the woman known as the Yellow Swan. She was—"

"I know who she was," he said, interrupting me. He wrinkled his forehead. "We all knew the lady — and I'm using the term *lady* generously. You couldn't help knowing her even if you wanted to avoid her." He shook his head as if he was not pleased with the thought of having known her.

"She used to come to our club after she finished her sets at the Cathay. I suppose she thought she was honoring us by slumming. She'd stay until dawn when we closed, if we let her stay, that is, if we didn't throw her out before then."

This was not the picture of the Yellow Swan I had in my mind. I decided to feign naiveté to see how this would play out.

"I know she was very popular," I said, as I smiled my most innocent smile, "and that she had great fans at the Tower Club. I suppose that crowd followed her here, too, after hours."

The bookkeeper shook his head. "Not unless they were Japanese. Occidentals and Chinese are not welcome here. We discourage them from coming in. If they're smart, they get the message pretty quickly and leave, or, if they stay, they don't come back another time."

He slowly shook his head as if recalling something unpleasant. "That's the way it is."

He said, "I can tell you this much, my friend. You don't know nothing about her if all you know is how she seemed on stage at the Cathay. She was wild, even by Shanghai standards.

"We banned her twice — maybe even more times — from our club, but relented every time, to our regret, when she promised she would clean up her act and straighten herself out, would stop causing disruptions for our other patrons."

That shocked me. This was not the Yellow Swan I'd envisioned. "Why would you ban—"

"Let's have a drink," the bookkeeper said. He quickly swiveled around on his chair and reached over to a shelf behind him. He grabbed two bottles of *Clover* beer from behind his desk, and handed one bottle to me.

I pulled the cap off the bottle, using an opener-tool he handed me. We clinked bottles, wished each other good *joss,* and nodded at one another. The beer tasted delicious. I was glad to have a long pull on it because I was very warm, but I put the bottle down on the desk after just one swig. I was anxious to get back to what he'd just told me.

Before I could ask another question, he answered my first one.

"The quiet, supposedly demur young woman her fans at the hotel and the newspapers seemed to adore, the young woman they thought they knew from her Tower Club act, the woman you obviously think you know from your investigation, would transform herself into a calculating, ill-tempered, hard woman once our doors closed behind her, and once she began her evening's regimen of alcohol, cocaine or opium."

He grinned as if about to impart some great secret, then added, "Here's somethin' else I bet you didn't know." He nodded. "She fraternized with Japanese businessmen and soldiers, as well as Japanese women.

"Does that surprise you?" he asked. "She was wanton with all them, sometimes publically in the club's entertaining room on the dance floor or at a table," he added, shaking his head in obvious disapproval of the Yellow Swan's brazen behavior.

I said I didn't know that.

"And here's something else, my friend," he said, furtively glancing around his office as if he was about to let me in on a great, secret conspiracy. "She sometimes worked the room as a flower-seller girl, not caring if her clients were men or women, or who knew about that. She was indiscriminate."

CHAPTER 39

THE PRESENT

Pock-Marked Huang bowed before Big-Eared Tu, then sat in a chair in the Great Room facing him across a small table. He waited to speak until the serving coolie left the room and Tu had taken a slurping swallow of tea.

"The former policeman has visited an after-hours club the Yellow Swan often went to when she finished her work at the hotel," Huang said.

"He also visited her apartment building owned by the Round-Eyes, Victor Sassoon, and visited the Tower Club itself. He talked to an employee." Huang waited for Tu to speak, but Tu remained silent.

"We, too, have now visited those places and know what the former policeman learned from his efforts." He relayed this information to Tu. "He did not learn much, Master Tu," Huang added, smiling as he said this.

"He also tried to find out information about the woman's history before she arrived in Shanghai. Again, he has not discovered much, although he did learn, through his Elder Brother, Ling Sun-yu, her true name and that she came here from Peking.

"It seems, Master Tu, that except for a brief run-in with a Dwarf Bandit JMP inspector detective who is investigating the same case, the former policeman has not yet provoked the Dwarf Bandits and has not risked causing an incident with them. For now, it seems, our business is not threatened by his investigation."

Tu picked up his tea bowl and slurped more tea. He then sat silently, contemplating what Huang had told him.

"*Ayeeyah!*" he said, after a few minutes. "It seems the former policeman does not need our assistance, but I want you to continue your observation of him.

"Be prepared to step in immediately to put an end to his investigation if he is about to provoke the Dwarf Bandits or, if necessary, put a quiet end to him if it seems the Dwarf Bandits will use his investigation as an excuse to take an action that might harm our business."

Huang bowed his head to acknowledge Tu's instructions. Then he said, "There is one more thing, Master Tu. Someone, a Dwarf Bandit, has been watching the former policeman. He follows him day and night."

"Kwantung? A soldier?" Tu asked.

Huang shook his head. "Not military as far as I can tell. He moves with the stealth of a martial arts warrior, but not one who is trained as a military person, not one who is in uniform, at least."

Tu again slurped his tea as he stared across the room. He gazed at his caged lucky crickets.

"Perhaps it is time for us to make our own inquiries in Peking about the woman they called the Yellow Swan. Possibly there was more to her than it seems."

CHAPTER 40

THE RECENT PAST: 1936

THE YELLOW SWAN FINISHED HER third Tower Club set of the evening, left the stage, and walked over to a table occupied by a middle-aged Chinese man. He seemed, based on his grooming and his conservative, western-style dress, to be a businessman.

She settled in at the table and waited to speak until the waiter filled her flute with champagne and had left.

"How have you been, Mr. Min," she said. "I have wondered why I haven't seen you for several weeks. Are you angry with the Yellow Swan for some reason?"

"*Ayeeyah!* No, my dear, I could never be angry with you. I have been in Canton on business, but have now come home to stay for a while and to spend glorious time with my Yellow Swan."

The Yellow Swan smiled over the top of her glass and nodded once. Her eyes locked on Min's eyes.

"That makes me very content. I am happy you will be here to visit me," she said. "I have missed you."

Min nodded. "Do you still love me or have you found some other wealthy lover during my absence?"

"There is no one for me but you, Mr. Min, not ever. The Yellow Swan does not share her limited affection or special favors with anyone but you."

Min smiled, and thought, *You dare lie to me, you whore!* Then he reached out, smiled, and lightly squeezed the Yellow Swan's hand.

She was exhausted from her evening with Min. But, nevertheless, she left her apartment after he'd gone home, and rode a taxi to the grandfathered Cherry Blossom Club in Hongkew.

The Yellow Swan shared a table in a dark corner of the entertaining room with a Japanese colonel in the Kwantung army.

"You are a delight, as always, to see and a delight to spend time with, my dear," the officer said. "I am honored to be in your presence, my dear Yellow Swan."

"The honor is mine, Colonel," the Yellow Swan said. "I am always happy to share my evenings with a hero of the Emperor's army."

CHAPTER 41

DAY TWO OF THE INVESTIGATION

WHEN I LEFT THE MAJESTIC Café, I headed to Chapei to visit the Del Monte Cabaret, another club that had been grandfathered to stay open after-hours. This was the second club Elder Brother's triad source had mentioned to him.

This club had a policy of discouraging Dwarf Bandits and Round-Eyes from using its facilities, although it employed stunning Round-Eyes, White Russian women as its taxi dancers and flower-seller girls. The club tried to cater only to Chinese men and women.

Much to the distress of its manager and regular Chinese patrons, the club recently found itself in the situation where it was not able to enforce its restrictive policy against Kwantung soldiers and officers, who insisted on using the club for their pleasure. The Dwarf Bandits, the club's manager would soon tell me, swaggered about the club, became belligerent, and threw around their weight. It seemed, he told me, as if they believed that the club, as well as the city, would soon be theirs to do with whatever they wanted.

———◆———

The Del Monte Cabaret was located at the foot of a small wooden bridge near Soochow Creek, where the creek met the Whangpoo.

The Del Monte Cabaret was not really a nightclub, not a true cabaret, in spite of its name, since it did not focus on musical or dance entertainment for its customers. The Del Monte actually was a gambling club that offered roulette, chemin de fer, and craps on its top three floors. But as a hook to bring in business, the club also provided White Russian female companions on its ground floor for its men and women customers.

The Del Monte was located in a four-story, free standing building — what the inspector detectives in the SMP commonly referred to as a roadhouse café. The building itself was not too old — I'd guess about ten years old — so that by Chapei's standards, it was almost brand new. The painted outside walls still looked fresh.

The inside lights were dimmed, so I couldn't really appraise the actual condition of the entertaining room as I entered it. I could only see what the nighttime patrons would see.

Much to my surprise, each of the dozen or so tables scattered around the room had a white table cloth on it. This was more upscale than I'd anticipated. Like the Majestic Café, however, the Del Monte smelled from stale cigarette smoke, stale opium, used linen, Brilliantine, and flower-seller girls' cheap perfume.

The club had several closed doors spread around the entertaining room. I couldn't tell which one was the club's special entrance, the door most clubs offered as an accommodation to men who did not want to be seen entering or leaving the building. One other wall was lined with four closed doors that typically hid private rooms used for secret assignations.

The Del Monte Cabaret was well-known for its pre-dawn

ham and eggs, its generously poured glasses of alcohol, and its attractive White Russian women waitresses — known collectively as *Natashas* — who also served the club's customers as taxi dancers and flower-seller girls when not handling tables.

Its music was performed by a small band of local expatriate American and British jazzmen. The band's repertoire featured popular American film and Broadway show tunes as well as some jazz. The music was internally broadcast over speakers strategically placed around the entertaining room.

"The Yellow Swan was very popular here," the manager, a South African Occidental Round-Eyes, in his late forties, said to me. "She will be gravely missed by our workers and customers."

That's an interesting contrast to what I heard at the Majestic, I thought.

"Did she use drugs here," I asked, "or tend to drink too much alcohol?"

The manager shrugged. "Who's to say what's too much? I only consider it too much if the user becomes a problem for our patrons, which she never did. Otherwise, it's Shanghai, in here, too, isn't it? Cocaine, opium, and booze are our city's currency."

He shrugged again and raised one eyebrow, as if to say, *You should know already this as a Shanghainese.*

I followed up on a statement he'd just made.

"Did the Yellow Swan ever become a problem?" I asked. "Did you ever have to insist she leave the club or did you ever ban her or threaten to ban her because she behaved badly?"

He squinted and shook his head as if surprised I'd asked these questions. "Why would you ask that?" he said. "I just said she never caused trouble. She was always a perfect lady. We always welcomed her here, as did our customers."

I wasn't ready to let go of this. "No problems, then, from her?" I said. "Not even after she'd been using drugs or drinking late into the night or early morning?"

"No, not ever. Why are you still asking these questions?"

"Just trying to get a full picture of her, that's all."

Based on the frown he cast at me, I wasn't sure he believed me, but he answered my question anyway.

"Not even once. In fact, the more dope she used or alcohol she drank, the sweeter she became. When she was under the influence, she often would spontaneously stand up by her table and sing along with the band. She knew all the latest American tunes, you know.

"Our customers and employees loved it when she did that. Yes, the Yellow Swan was a lovely young woman. She'll be sorely missed here."

"Did she fraternize with any of the Dwarf Bandit soldiers or officers who insisted on coming into the club, or just with the Chinese?" I said.

"Just the Chinese. Even though these days, under the rules of their military, we cannot keep those Jap blokes from our club, we have an unspoken rule that the races don't mix in here. The Yellow Swan always followed that rule."

"One last thing," I said. "Did she ever work here as a flower-seller girl?"

He looked stunned and clearly offended by my question. "Of course not." He shook his head and crossed his arms.

"Why would you ask that? The Yellow Swan was not a *ghee*

niu — a sing-song girl. She was a talented, vocal performer who often generously shared her talent when visiting us.

"She was not a part of the Flowery Kingdom," he added. He frowned and squinted. "Why would you think otherwise?" He seemed angry now.

"I need to get back to work," he said, as he abruptly stood up from his chair, almost knocking it over.

I walked home. I was totally confused. I'd been given diametrically opposed information about the Yellow Swan from two sources, both who should have known her, in general, or who should have known her, specifically, within the context of their own limited club environments.

There seemed to be two Yellow Swans: One who lived a decorous life as an upscale nightclub singer and after-hours patron of Chinese entertainment society; and, one who lived a fast-paced, drug and alcohol infused after-hours life in one of the city's notorious, raucous clubs, mixing with the city's Dwarf Bandit enemies.

The two Yellow Swans were hard to reconcile.

Day Two of my investigation was not progressing well. It seemed every time I found or received a good lead, something would come along to block or undermine it.

After I left the Del Monte, I stopped in the lobby of the nearby Astor House Hotel to use one of the telephones available to its room guests and restaurant patrons. Even though it was late in the day, I called Chief Inspector Chapman, sending him the signal to meet again. I wanted to bring him up to date on what I'd learned. His thoughts might prove helpful to me. And, of course, he would see that I was following his order that I report frequently to him.

CHAPTER 42

DAY TWO OF THE INVESTIGATION

C HIEF INSPECTOR CHAPMAN AND I met at our usual place. It was 6:00 p.m.

I told the chief inspector that since the Yellow Swan arrived in Shanghai in 1934, she'd lived at the Broadway Mansions, and that she frequented two after-hours clubs. I reminded him again that she socialized with both Chinese and Dwarf Bandit men and women. I told him, too, that she seemed to be more than a casual user of cocaine and opium, not to mention alcohol.

The chief inspector nodded. "Obviously, Old Boy, some of this we already know, Sun-jin, but now give me the details on everything. Don't leave anything out. Maybe I'll spot something you missed or that hadn't occurred to me before."

I set out all I knew for him. I did not, however, tell him my sources for some of the information, since doing that would have made it clear to him I had violated his order not to disclose my investigation to anyone else. Elder Brother's role in this, and the help he received from his triad sources, would have to remain unstated.

When I finished, he lit his pipe and vigorously puffed a few puffs. He was particularly interested in the different roles the Yellow Swan had assumed at the two after-hours nightclubs.

"That's a surprise," he said, "based on what you heard before from that pageboy, but not a surprise, either."

I knew exactly what he meant. People in Shanghai often lived contradictory lives, depending on where in the city they were or with whom they were spending their time.

"An entertainer using coke or opium, hanging out at after-hours clubs, occasionally becoming a disruption, isn't exactly a news story," he said. "This is Shanghai, after all."

"She offered a different image in public," I said. "Someone innocent and pure. I suppose she had to do that to create her business persona."

"Well, yes, perhaps. A better image for business," the chief inspector said, "or maybe that image really was her, not made up for public consumption, but then she would let herself go at the after-hours club for some reason we don't know about. It wouldn't be the first time in the performance business, Old Boy."

I shrugged. "Who's to say?" I was skeptical. I thought there probably was more to the Yellow Swan's conflicting personalities than letting herself go from her business, but I was not going to press the point with the chief inspector.

"I wonder how she could afford the apartment at the Broadway Mansions?" I said, testing the water on this point. I knew the chief inspector would order me to back off this line of thought because of Sassoon's likely involvement, if I made myself too clear to him.

"Probably the usual way," he answered, not picking up on my real direction on this point. "She likely was a kept woman."

I paused and considered my next statement.

I decided to press this point after all. It was clear the chief inspector had no idea I was referring to Sassoon.

"Then I need to find out who was keeping her there," I said. "He should be my number-one suspect in this homicide, at least for now."

Nothing. No reaction from the chief inspector to my statement or to its implicit accusation.

"One other thing, Old Boy," Chapman said.

"Sir?"

"SMP investigator Ma Wang knows you have been around the crime scene asking questions, although he doesn't know who you are. You need to be more careful or you'll be discovered."

I felt my neck and shoulders stiffen. I counted to five to tame my rising anger.

"*Ayeeyah!* Sir, how am I to investigate this case, with all the restrictions you've imposed on me, if I cannot even visit the crime scene and interview witnesses?"

"I'm not saying you cannot do those things, Sun-jin. I'm not a fool. I'm just saying, Old Boy, you need to be mindful that Inspector Detective Ma is aware of your presence. He will undoubtedly be on the lookout for you."

I nodded. "I'll play-up my cover story if it's necessary. I don't see what else I can do and still be able to investigate the crime."

"Tell me what your cover story is?" the chief inspector said.

"It's simple, sir. I'm a devoted fan who has decided to write a tribute story about the Yellow Swan, and sell it through Mickey Hahn, the Round-Eyes reporter, to her newspaper to publish."

"Good," the chief inspector said.

"My story should appease Inspector Detective Ma, should explain to him why I met with the pageboy, and why I am asking questions about the Yellow Swan," I said. "Hopefully, he won't be suspicious if he hears I'm nosing around."

"It should work," Chapmen said, "but your cover story means you brought that Emily Hahn person into the picture. I told you not to tell anyone about your investigation."

"I didn't tell her anything about the case or my investigation. I merely said I was a serious fan of the Yellow Swan, was deeply saddened by her sudden, violent death, and wanted to write a testimonial to her for all the other Yellow Swan fans.

"We agreed I would write the story on speculation, either for her newspaper or for *The New Yorker* magazine in America — her choice, since Hahn works in Shanghai for both publications — with no guarantee either publication would buy the article. Of course, I don't care if they buy it or not since it's only a ruse.

"Hahn was enthusiastic about the idea, and said the story would be more appropriate for the Shanghai newspaper's audience than for the United States weekly magazine since it was likely no one in America has ever heard of the Yellow Swan. She has no reason to suspect the authenticity of my cover story."

Chapman smiled and nodded. "Good. Very good. Very clever, Old Boy. Do what you must, but don't be caught, and do solve the crime before the week is out."

I nodded, but didn't comment. As if I needed reminding by him.

CHAPTER 43

DAY TWO OF THE INVESTIGATION

HEADED HOME FROM MY MEETING with Chief Inspector Chapman, cooked and ate supper, and settled at the kitchen table with the Murder Book opened in front of me. Bik, who had eaten the leftover food from my dinner, laid curled on the floor under the table. She snored softly.

As the second day of my investigation came to an end, I thought about the time restraint I was operating under and what I must do to accelerate my progress.

I considered what I'd learned so far about the Yellow Swan. I now knew her true name, her approximate age, when she arrived in Shanghai, where she'd come from, her sometimes demur personality as part of her business image, her sometimes seemingly contradictory night life, her drug habit, and her occasional foray into the world of the Flowery Kingdom. I also found it interesting that in one after-hours club she fraternized only with Dwarf Bandit men and women, and in the other club only with Chinese men and women. What I didn't know yet was how, if at all, these disparate facts and her practices might have led to her death.

This information meant that the groups of possible suspects

had now widened to include fellow entertainers, jealous men or women, drug dealers or users, members of the Kwantung army in Shanghai, and members of the opposing Chinese Nationalist KMT army in Shanghai.

All this to be sorted out and evaluated as the clock ticked away and wound down on my investigation.

CHAPTER 44

THE PRESENT

KANJI LOCKED THE DOOR OF the hut he was living in while in Hongkew, then stripped to his waist, reveling his intricate collection of body ink. He lowered himself to the dirt floor, crossed his legs, and sat before the shrine he'd created to honor Matsuko in her death.

He had everything he would need to pay proper Shinto respect, in her death, to the woman he had loved during her life. He had a sampling of Matsuko's ashes he'd been given by her father; he had a small, but several years-old photograph of Matsuko; he had incense sticks to burn; and had a bucket of water — *taoke* — and a water dipper — *hishaku* — with which he would purify her replica gravestone — her *haka*.

His personal offering — always optional under the ritual — would be a small vile of his own blood which he would pour over the *haka*, demonstrating his respect for his fallen lover.

Kanji sat before Matsuko's shrine, his head bowed, contemplating Matsuko's brief life in this world. The Buddhist in him said that her death was acceptable, that it was merely one step on her journey to salvation. The Shintoist in him said that her death was the start of a dark, unpleasant journey for his lover.

Kanji thought, *I honored Matsuko in life; now I will honor her in death by performing this scared ritual. Then I will again honor Matsuko by avenging her murder. I am ready.*

CHAPTER 45

THE RECENT PAST: 1936

"YOU MUST OBEY ME, MEI-HUA," Colonel Wu Lin-feng said. "The times are not as modern as you would like to think. Not everyone believes it is appropriate for a KMT colonel's daughter to engage in treasonous acts so she can seem modern. You must publicly renounce your previous relationship with the communist bandits.

"That is not all, Daughter. You must give up your former policeman. We cannot have you involved with someone who is *low faan — not full-blooded Chinese, a mongrel.* The important people in the KMT will frown upon such a demeaning relationship.

Mei-hua shrugged. "Is that what you think, Father? Are those your wishes or are those the wishes of your superiors?

"Mine, Daughter. This reflects my wishes."

"Then you miss the point of my activities, Father. I have not participated in strikes and boycotts, or walked the Long March, and I am not involved with Sun-jin, so I can seem to be modern. I have done all these things because I *am* modern.

"Chiang and the KMT's days are as passé, Father, as are the archaic viewpoints of the Manchu."

Mei-hua turned toward her mother, who stood behind Wu Lin-feng.

"Mother, do you agree with father? Do you believe I should end my romance with Sun-jin, and renounce my prior political opinions and activity?"

"I believe you are endangering yourself and our family," her mother said, "even though that is not your intent."

Mei-hua frowned. She felt her back stiffen. She looked into her mother's eyes. She hadn't expected that response.

"And I think the days when a father and mother can order their adult daughter to live a life of seclusion, and not associate with ideas and with the people she wants to associate with, have passed. That is what Sun Yat-sen's overthrow of the Manchu Dynasty and the founding of the Republic were all about."

She paused and stared at her parents, first one, then the other.

"Otherwise, when I was born, you should have just cast me off, should have left me in the Baby Drawer to be found and raised by the Round-Eyes missionaries, or maybe left me on a hillside to die. That would have been my preference."

CHAPTER 46

THE PRESENT

BIG-EARED TU SLOWLY WALKED TEN meters in front of three young men whose sole mission in life was to guard him from harm whenever he left his French Concession home. Pock-Marked Huang walked alongside him.

Tu gripped the side of his olive-green mandarin gown in his left hand, pulling the hem up slightly so he would not step on it as he walked on the uneven, brick sidewalk. In his other hand, he held a small wooden bird cage.

Tu, following an old, established Shanghai tradition, was taking his prized lucky songbird — a young sparrow — for its daily, early-morning walk, one hour after sunrise. He would soon meet with other old men at the Baby Wall near the Whangpoo River in the Settlement. There, the old men would drink tea, smoke cigarettes, exchange the most recent gossip, and talk about songbirds. Tu valued this tradition because the long walks from his home to the Baby Wall and then back home again were his only respite each day from business.

Once assembled, the old men freed their swallows from their cages and watched them soar toward the clouds. The light, small wooden pennywhistles attached to the birds' tails made a distinctive sound as the birds climbed to gain altitude, and as the air rushed through the tiny wooden instruments.

This practice usually lasted thirty or so minutes before the old men whistled-in their lucky songbirds, and the pets reliably returned to their cages.

Tu waited until his songbird had flown out of sight before he turned to Huang.

"What have you learned about the Dwarf Bandit who follows the former policeman?"

"He is a Yakuza from Shanghai. He is assisting a Yakuza from Peking. The Peking Dwarf Bandit's name is Kanji Gorō."

"Why does he follow the former inspector detective?"

"Gorō was the singing woman's lover — the Yellow Swan's lover — when she lived in Peking. Our associates there tell me he has sworn to avenge her death, and has come to Shanghai to do so."

Tu nodded. "He could provoke the Dwarf Bandits into finding an incident, even though that would not be his intent."

Tu gazed up at the sky, searching for his songbird. It was not in sight.

"Does he believe Sun-jin murdered the Yellow Swan? Is that why he follows him?" Tu said.

"I don't yet know, Master Tu. He either believes that and will seek his revenge against Sun-jin or he hopes the former policeman's investigation will lead him to the killer."

Tu said nothing. He reached into a fold inside his Mandarin gown and extracted a small, wooden whistle from a pocket. He looked up, placed the end of the whistle against his lips and blew into it. He continued to stare at the sky.

After half a minute, Tu smiled and pointed his hand toward the sky.

"There," he said, as he gestured toward a small black speck in the sky. He laughed and nodded several times, watching as the spot became larger as it approached him and Huang.

"My reliable, lucky songbird returns to its cage."

CHAPTER 47

THE RECENT PAST: 1936

THE YELLOW SWAN WAS TIRED. Her three sets at the Tower Club had been unusually strenuous and draining this night. A fight — something that had never happened before in her presence at the club — had broken out among three young Round-Eyes men. Two of them fought, they claimed, to defend her honor when she refused the insistent requests of the other member of their group that she sing the song *Violets For Your Furs* for the third time in the same set.

When the Yellow Swan politely refused, having already twice indulged the young man by repeating the song to meet his requests, the young man threw his drink at her, soaking the front of her dress. The Yellow Swan left the small stage to change clothes and to avoid the likely outburst that followed. She returned to the stage, nervous and stressed, when the SMP uniformed constables arrived and took the three men into custody.

When her work finished for the night, the Yellow Swan boarded a rickshaw and instructed the coolie-puller to take her to the Del Monte Cabaret.

She sat alone, off to a side of the entertaining room, far from the lights of the bandstand, cloaked in the darkness of low lighting and shadows cast by nearby wooden pillars. She drank bar-rail champagne from a sturdy flute.

Forty-five minutes passed. She consumed three flutes of champagne. Her eyes never left the table top.

She looked up at the sound of the entrance door opening, sat up straight when she saw who had entered the club, and smoothed her lap with her palms, as the Nationalist KMT colonel spotted her and crossed the floor, coming quickly over to her.

"I'm grateful to see you, my dear," the colonel said to the Yellow Swan, as he pulled out a chair and sat down across the table from her.

The Yellow Swan smiled demurely, slightly lowering her chin toward her chest and fluttering her eye lashes, as she looked up at the officer across from her.

"The pleasure is all mine, colonel Wu. As always."

"It will be a while before we see each other again," he said, "so we must make tonight one we shall not forget."

The Yellow Swan reflexively pouted as she wondered why the colonel and she would not be together for some time after tonight. That could be valuable information to know.

"*Ayeeyah*," she said, "that is very bad news, bad *joss*. I will miss you, Colonel."

"And I will miss you, but the life of a soldier is unpredictable, you know."

The Yellow Swan recognized this opportunity to acquire information for her father.

"We must drink, then, Colonel, to your quick and safe return to Shanghai, and to our rendezvous when you have returned." She raised her flute in a contrived toast.

"To my colonel. May you speedily and safely return to your Yellow Swan from . . . from . . . from where, Colonel? You haven't told me. How can I properly toast you without knowing that?"

"From leading the Nineteenth Route Army as it chases the bandit, Mao Tse-tung, away from Shanghai, to wherever fortune might take us until we capture or kill him," Wu said.

The Yellow Swan smiled and nodded. "Let us drink to that, then, Colonel, and then let us head back to the Broadway Mansions to pillow and to share a night we both will recall with pleasure until you return to the Yellow Swan from your excursion after the bandits."

CHAPTER 48

DAY THREE OF THE INVESTIGATION

DAY THREE ARRIVED.

I was awakened early in the morning by the sound of Bik barking, growling, and scratching with her paw at the front door with such ferocity that it seemed she might want to rush through the closed door to reach whoever was on the other side of it.

I looked at my watch. It was almost time to get up and engage in my daily practice of *Shaolin*.

When I went to the living room to see the cause of her agitation, Bik turned and looked at me, then turned back to the door and growled again. I hadn't heard her growl since that day two years ago when I found her in the copse of trees overlooking the Baby Wall.

I grabbed a thick bamboo stick I keep near the door to use for protection, if necessary. I paused briefly, then yanked the door open.

JMP Inspector Detective Harue stood there looking very annoyed.

"*Hai!* Call off your mutt before I blow off its head. I will take steps to protect myself," he said. His hand rested on the butt of his holstered pistol.

Without inviting Harue into my apartment, I leaned over and grabbed Bik's collar. I walked her back to my bedroom and closed the door to keep her in. Then I returned to Harue, who still stood in the hallway, scowling and looking in.

"*Ayeeyah.* Come in, Inspector Detective," I said, as I motioned him through the doorway with a slow sweep of my hand. I stepped aside to give him room to pass by me. I made sure he saw the bamboo stick I'd been holding as I returned it to its place in the corner, leaning against the wall.

"Early for you to be calling on me, isn't it, Inspector Detective?"

"I warned you not to investigate the death of the Yellow Swan," Harue said, "that it was now an Imperial Japanese police and military matter. You didn't listen."

I kept quiet to see where he would go with this.

"You are under arrest for interfering with my investigation," he said. "Come with me to my station house."

He held out a pair of handcuffs and motioned for me to place my hands behind my back and turn around so he could restrain my wrists.

"*Bú — No.*" I said. I shook my head. "You've got it all wrong. I wasn't investigating the murder or trying to solve the crime. I didn't interfere with your investigation."

"*Hai!* What were you doing at the Broadway Mansions and at the Tower Club?"

"Working on a freelance newspaper story about the Yellow Swan for the *North-China Daily News*. Gathering background information about the young woman so I can write an article for the society page of the newspaper. I plan to sell it to that

American reporter who works there, that Round-Eyes Mickey Hahn woman.

"*Ayeeyah!* You should talk to her," I said. "She'll tell you we have an arrangement where she'll buy my story for the paper if she likes it. It has nothing to do with your investigation."

"Why did you tell a pageboy at the Cathay he could not speak with me because I am not the official investigator. That interfered with my investigation," Harue said.

"I did no such thing. I don't know anything about that. Why would I do that? It makes no sense. Think about it."

Harue frowned. I could see that my reasonable explanation had thrown him off balance and probably had upset the plans he had for me this morning. He obviously came here expecting to arrest me.

Would he buy my cover story?

He put away the handcuffs, clipping them to his belt.

"*Hai!* I'll check on this," he said. "If you're lying to me, I'll be back."

I know you will, I thought.

CHAPTER 49

THE RECENT PAST: 1936

NOTWITHSTANDING HIS BEST INTENTION NOT to return to Shanghai from Peking, Kanji found himself in Hongkew again, outside the after-hours nightclub, the Cherry Blossom, watching for Matsuko to leave when it closed. He planned to follow her home — if she went home.

This was his second night secretly in Shanghai. He'd come there at the suggestion of his Yakuza brother, who had reported events to Kanji that suggested Matsuko had lost her way with the Code of Bushido.

The sun was close to rising. Birds were beginning to chirp, insects beginning to swarm. The night-soil collectors passed by, pushing their heavy carts toward the Whangpoo to dump their fetid contents into the river.

Kanji knew the club would be closing in the next few minutes and that Matsuko would finally emerge.

Alone, this time, he hoped.

————◆————

Kanji followed her home and hid outside for several hours until the Chinese colonel she'd brought home with her left the building. Then he pushed the buzzer to her apartment, tapped his foot as he waited for Matsuko to answer, and pushed the buzzer again. Then . . . a few seconds later, again.

"*Ayeeyah!* Who's there? Go away," Matsuko's voice said, crackling though the intercom speaker. "Come back later after lunch."

Kanji leaned his thumb on the buzzer and did not lift it this time until she answered again.

"Leave me alone, whoever you are," Matsuko said.

"It is me, Matsuko-san. Unlock the front door so I can come up."

Kanji strode through the door she held open, not removing his sandals. He brushed past Matsuko without saying a word to her. He pushed into the living room. He did not take a seat, but turned back to face her as she entered the room. His legs were spaced his shoulders' width apart.

"Why are you here, Kanji-san?"

"You are pillowing with Celestials," he said. "You are a disgrace to Bushido and your father and ancestors."

"No, I have not. I would never dishonor my father and ancestors by doing that."

"I saw you, Matsuko-san."

"Are you spying on me again?" she asked. She narrowed her eyes. They became hard, cold, and flinty.

"I do what I must to learn information to assist the Emperor. There is no shame in that."

"There is shame in your methods," Kanji said. "You must give up this life and return with me to the home of your father."

"What I do is none of your business," she said. "Now, leave

my home and leave me alone. Do not bother me again." She briefly paused. "Not ever!"

She walked to the entry door and held it open. She looked hard at Kanji. "Go now," she said. "Do not return."

Kanji did not move. "You have been with a Celestial. I have seen you with my own eyes. You are shameless."

"Lies," Matsuko said. "It was not me you saw. You did not see me because I am never with Celestials. You are lying or mistaken. Now leave."

CHAPTER 50

THE PRESENT

"YOU MUST TAKE CARE, SUN-JIN. My father is a dangerous man."

Mei-hua and I were in bed, enjoying a rare day when the air outside was not an acrid, brown mist. The sun glimmered through the window, warming the bedroom. Bik was curled up by our feet, on top of the blanket that covered us.

"I'm aware of that, Mei-hua, that the warnings of any KMT officer should not be taken lightly, but I will not stop my relationship with you so he can become a general. Not unless you want to end our relationship." I shook my head and laughed.

"Does that fool of your father really believe I'm blocking his promotion by being with you?"

Mei-hua nodded and rolled her eyes. "*Ayeeyah!* He's frustrated, and I understand his concern. It's not entirely without basis. I'm his current excuse why he has not been promoted," she said.

"My father believes my former CCP affiliation, and now my relationship with a former policeman who also is *low faan*, have been barriers to his advancement. He forgets that before I knew you and before it became known that I was active in the CCP, he'd been passed over for promotion several times."

"*Shi. — Yes.*" I shook my head. "Then that settles it," I said. "I do not have to perform a humanitarian act and lose the love of my life, since it appears doing so will not help him in any event." I laughed again.

"Be wary, Sun-jin. Do not underestimate how dangerous my father can be. He is ruthless and unpredictable. Whether he is right or not, he is formidable and can be treacherous. I worry about you."

"I can take care of myself. I left the SMP, Mei-hua, but I did not relinquish my skills or experience. I will take care of myself."

CHAPTER 51

THE PRESENT

"OUR ASSOCIATES IN PEKING HAVE been most helpful, Master Tu," Pock-Marked Huang said. He and Big-Eared Tu sat in Tu's Great Room.

Tu tapped his foot behind the hem of his gown. He was growing tired of this matter involving the former policeman. It seemed the policeman's investigation was not making progress, but, more importantly, was not stirring up the Kwantung Dwarf Bandits. So, why bother continuing?

Perhaps I have worried about this for nothing, Tu thought.

"The woman's father, as you know, is a minor functionary in the Dwarf Bandit embassy in Peking. More importantly, Master Tu, what perhaps you did not know, is that he is a spy for the Kwantung. He uses his diplomatic position to cover his treachery against we Chinese."

Tu smiled for the first time that day. His smile, as always, was fraught with unstated danger toward whomever he directed it. Huang worried his report had stirred something dangerous against him in Tu's mind.

"Was the *low faan* woman also a spy?" Tu said.

"It is hard to tell. We don't know that, not yet, but we do

know she often fraternized with both Dwarf Bandits and with Chinese military men, so perhaps she was."

"Then perhaps her treachery was the motive for her death," Tu said. "Attempt to learn more along this path from our Peking brothers."

CHAPTER 52

THE PRESENT

MEI-HUA WAS FRUSTRATED.

Her burning desire to aid the cause of the CCP as a spy — especially now that she no longer was openly active in the Revolution — remained only a hope for her. So far, she had not learned any information about the KMT that might be useful to the CCP's military.

This was not from lack of trying. Every day, Mei-hua read all the KMT-leaning Shanghai newspapers - the *North-China Daily News,* the *Shanghai Times,* the *Evening Post and Mercury,* and the *North-China Herald,* among others — looking for hidden or unintended leads that would suggest information to her she could pass onto the CCP. She always came up empty.

Her former comrades in the CCP, those former conspirators to whom she'd foolishly bragged that she would be a spy one day on behalf of the Revolution since she no longer could be a visible participant, now avoided her, even laughed at her when they could not avoid her, candidly reminding Mei-hua that she had not yet fulfilled her promise to the Revolution.

"You really should stay home, Mei-hua and tend to your mother's house," said one person. "That is your true calling.

You are not cut out for the Revolution. You never did have your heart in it, not even when you played at the role of someone participating in the Long March." He paused, then said, "How far did you say you got before you dropped out and returned to your comfortable, bourgeois middle-class life?"

CHAPTER 53

DAY THREE OF THE INVESTIGATION

CHIEF INSPECTOR CHAPMAN AND I met again.

At his insistence, I told him, once again, all I knew about the Yellow Swan, repeating much of what I'd told him before. This was becoming tedious, but he said this would give him full context. He was the boss in this assignment, so I repeated myself for him.

I also told him the obvious, told him what I had avoided telling him before, that I now believed Victor Sassoon was Matsuko's secret lover and benefactor. He still did not draw the obvious conclusion from that — that Sassoon therefore was a prime suspect in the Yellow Swan's death. I would explain this to him later, if necessary, when I could better defend this conclusion and deal with his response, since I knew he'd be upset by this. I still hoped that, given some time for the idea to take hold, he would arrive at that same conclusion himself, without me bringing it up.

I again described Inspector Detective Harue's early-morning visit to me.

"I'm concerned about Harue," the chief inspector said. "Do you think he believed your cover story?"

I nodded. "Otherwise he would have arrested me and hauled me in to his station house. That's what he came to do in the first place."

"Will the Hahn woman confirm your story if Harue checks up on it?"

"Yes. She believes it's true," I said.

Chapman pulled on his pipe. "Time's running out, Sun-jin. Are you going to wrap this up in the next day or two?"

"I'm doing what I can."

"Are you really any closer to solving this than you were the last time we talked?"

"Yes and no. I now have some meaningful categories of suspects," I said. I told the chief inspector about drug dealers, to appease him, and also that I had identified one actual suspect I planned to interview later today.

"Who's that?" he asked.

"Victor Sassoon," I said.

I watched the color drain from the chief inspector's face.

CHAPTER 54

DAY THREE OF THE INVESTIGATION

T HE CHIEF INSPECTOR ABRUPTLY STOOD up. "Are you out of your mind, Sun-jin?"

His face was flushed. He scowled. "Don't you ever learn?" His body became rigid. "Do you even remember why I fired you?" His voice had elevated in volume and pitch.

A fair few questions, I thought, *but no longer relevant.*

"Yes, sir, I do, but there's more to this than you might initially think. Hear me out."

The chief inspector sighed, letting out a long, slow breath.

"Okay. Explain yourself." He settled back into his chair, but his face remained dark. He set up his pipe, lit it, then furiously puffed on it.

"Take the fact that the Yellow Swan lived in a luxury apartment. We both know she couldn't afford that on her own, so, as you and I agreed last time we met, someone must have been subsidizing her. I haven't turned up anyone. Has *your* SMP investigator done any better?"

"No," he said. He blinked hard.

The chief inspector did not seem placated by my statements or question. His tone did not suggest I'd yet assuaged him.

"If your people and I both cannot find her benefactor," I said, "there's a good chance she was being allowed to live at the Broadway Mansions for free. If so, only the owner — Sassoon — could do that.

"Combine that with the fact that Sassoon was also her employer at the Tower Club. It all stands to reason that he—"

The chief inspector held up his palm and stopped me mid-sentence.

He slowly shook his head. His normal color returned to his face. He now seemed resigned to my position, or, at least, had given in and surrendered to it.

"Tread carefully, Sun-jin. As you know, Victor Sassoon is not a man to be trifled with. We both stand to come out of this badly if you're not careful and diplomatic."

"Yes, sir," I said. "How well I know that."

CHAPTER 55

DAY THREE OF THE INVESTIGATION

I USED MY MICKEY HAHN/*NORTH-CHINA DAILY News* cover story as a basis for making an appointment to see Victor Sassoon at his office in the Sassoon House on East Nanking Road. I was surprised he agreed to see me, but assumed that my use of Hahn's name when I requested the meeting played a positive role in his decision.

Sassoon and Hahn reputedly had been "on again, off again" lovers until she fell in love with the notorious Chinese poet, publisher, and opium addict, Zau Sinmay, and left Sassoon in the lurch so she could move in with Zau. Eventually, Hahn and Sassoon became just friends, although the fact that she lived with Zau reputedly continued to irritate Sassoon, based on public comments he made from time-to-time.

———◆———

"Why are you here, Mr. Ling?" Sassoon said to me as soon as his comprador, Chen Bao, showed me into Sassoon's office. "I know you no longer are employed by the Special Branch of the SMP."

"Please call me Sun-jin," I said. "I'm here on my own, Taipan, not as a cop."

Sassoon said nothing.

"I'm writing a story for Mickey Hahn to publish in the *North-China Daily News*. It's about Matsuko Akasuki — the Yellow Swan. Her fans hunger for information about the young woman — who she really was, where she came from, why she came to Shanghai, how she lived and survived in luxurious fashion on nothing but a singer's salary, and, of course, why she was murdered."

"As I said, Mr. Ling, why are you here?"

"Let's start with this. Will you tell me where she came from before Shanghai? There's no reason you shouldn't."

"Peking. Now, once again, why are you here?"

"I know you were her employer at the Tower Club, Taipan, and that she lived in your Broadway Mansions Apartments. Was she your lover, too? Did you subsidize her life style?"

"That's none of your business."

"Did you know she was a drug addict and occasionally worked as a flower-seller girl?"

Sassoon said nothing. Instead, he reached into a humidor sitting on top of his desk and removed a cigar. After clipping its end and lighting it, he said, "So what. She's dead and no longer works for me."

"Did you know she had relationships with Dwarf Bandit men and women, as well as Chinese men and women? Sexual relationships."

"Why would I care?"

"Because your name is associated with hers, and this will become public as soon as I publish my story."

Sassoon shrugged. "Only if Mickey Hahn is foolish and

decides to publish your story," he said. "She might not want to do that once I threaten her and the newspaper with a defamation law suit if they publish it."

Although I had anticipated this response, I was annoyed by it.

"*Kenong — Maybe.* My story is based on evidence, not rumor or conjecture, Taipan. You don't frighten me, and I doubt you will be able to frighten your friend, Miss Hahn, into not publishing it."

Sassoon's eyes narrowed. "If you continue to stick your nose where it doesn't belong," he said, "and if you publish the story, you will proceed at your own peril, Mr. Ling. I have great resources I will bring against you, resources you will not be able to defend against.

"Watch out what you write about me, who you talk to about me, and what you say or imply about me. I will not be trifled with and will not be defamed by the likes of you. I would think you would know that by now."

PART THREE

CHAPTER 56

DAY FOUR OF THE INVESTIGATION

THE DAY AFTER MY MEETING with Victor Sassoon, I sat in my kitchen thinking about the case, regrouping, and considering how I would approach my next step. Bik was sitting by the window, staring outside. Occasionally, she would briefly turn her head and look back at me. Then she would resume staring out the window.

I had only three days left to solve the murder and, hopefully, avoid an incident raised by the Dwarf Bandit's military before Chief Inspector Chapman dropped the hammer on me.

I thought about my meeting with Sassoon. Although he had not answered any of my questions other than to tell me where the Yellow Swan lived before she came to Shanghai, and, indeed, had threatened me with a defamation lawsuit and consequent ruin if I mentioned him and Mickey Hahn in my newspaper article, the meeting actually had been instructive.

Not only had I learned another piece of the puzzle — an important fact about the Yellow Swan's origin — but I also had rattled Sassoon, as evidenced by his abrupt threat made against me. Since I knew which specific questions I had intended to pose to him if he had allowed me to do so, questions he refused to answer by threatening me, I now also knew that each of these unasked questions might amount to a specific investigatory lead for me to follow, a lead Sassoon had seemed to anticipate by avoiding my questions and threatening me. Sassoon remained my prime suspect.

I thought about what I now knew and what my next step would be in my investigation.

I would start with the fact the Yellow Swan had lived in Peking before she moved to Shanghai.

I thought more, too, about the woman who had been the Yellow Swan — Matsuko Akasuki. I wanted to learn more about her background and her private life in both Peking And Shanghai, since what little I did know seemed to be so much at odds with her projected public persona offered at the Tower Club and at the Del Monte Cabaret.

There were other things I also wanted to learn about her, too.

I wondered, for example, why she consorted with both Chinese and Dwarf Bandit men and women, and why she acted differently with each group.

I made a mental note that some of the people she'd spent time with were KMT officers, but that others were Kwantung military officers.

Was it possible, I wondered, *that she had a secret agenda with respect to each group?*

Was the Yellow Swan a spy for one group or the other? Was she a double agent? Had she been murdered because she'd been a spy?

CHAPTER 57

THE PRESENT

MEI-HUA WAS THRILLED. SHE SMILED. *Maybe what her mother was telling her would be the* good *joss* — good luck — she hungered for.

"So," she said to her mother, "father is leading a company of KMT soldiers to take advantage of the distraction provided by the Dwarf Bandits' mobilization, and will attack the CCP at nearby Suzhou?"

"Quiet, Daughter!" her mother said, her eyes opening wide. She extended her finger and placed it against her lips. "Shhh! You must not say this out loud. The walls have ears. I should not have told you."

"The walls will not hear me speak of this again, Mother. I promise."

———⬥———

"Why should I believe this information?" the captain said. "You are the daughter of the enemy's colonel, a drop-out from our Revolution. How do I know you are not here to trick me, to have me lead my troops into an ambush?"

Mei-hua's neck and face warmed. She opened and closed

her fist without thinking about her action. She was furious. She had risked her life to bring this information to the CCP, her first delivery of information since she decided to spy against Chiang and the KMT. And now this officer had the impudence not to trust her.

"You will have to decide for yourself, Captain. I cannot make you believe me," she said. "If you do not want to fight my father's troops, then, at the least, leave here and protect your own troops.

"But, if you do abandon this post, I suggest you leave someone here to secretly watch this site. See if my father's men arrive to look for you. Decide then if I have told you the truth, and remember your conclusion for the future. I'll allow you only this one lapse of good judgement."

The captain stood up. "Guard," he shouted. When two soldiers entered his tent, he said, "Keep this woman in custody until we see if she is a spy for Chiang's bandits."

Two hours later, as the captain and his troops marched away from Suzhou, his rear cadre, who by then had left Suzhou, reported by short-wave radio that Wu Lin-feng's soldiers had come to the town, but had since left, probably because they hadn't found any enemy there.

"You are free to leave now," the captain said to Mei-hua. "I am sincerely grateful for your warning."

At last, Mei-hua thought, *I am a spy.*

CHAPTER 58

DAY FOUR OF THE INVESTIGATION

I VISITED BIG-EARED TU AGAIN. WE sat in his Great Room, as always, slurping tea while we talked.

"*Ayeeyah!* You are unyielding," Tu said. "I told you I will not help you."

I was now concerned I might be annoying him with my persistence. That was never a good idea with Tu, but I didn't have any other choice if I wanted to move forward with an idea I had to advance my investigation.

"Please reconsider, Master Tu. For the good of Shanghai, if not for your own good."

Tu shrugged slightly and remained silent.

"The Dwarf Bandits wish to provoke another incident. All the signs are there," I said, "including the build-up of troops and ships near the Bund. If we do not quickly solve the murder of the Yellow Swan, and demonstrate that her death was not sponsored by the Municipal Council or by Chiang's KMT or some ordinary Chinese-citizen criminal, we all will suffer from the combat that will follow when the Dwarf Bandits attack the city."

"Perhaps," Tu said. He reached over and indifferently flicked a crumb of food from his other sleeve.

I continued. "At the very least, the Dwarf Bandits will find some hapless Chinese person to blame for the murder and will use that as an excuse to bomb and invade Shanghai.

"I have a new piece of information that should be helpful to us," I said. "I have learned that the Yellow Swan lived in Peking before coming to Shanghai."

Tu remained silent.

It was time, I decided, to present my idea to Tu.

"I would like to fly to Peking tonight or tomorrow and meet with your colleagues to learn what they know about the Yellow Swan. Will you arrange that for me?"

Tu rang a bell to call his serving coolie. He ordered a second pot of tea for us.

When we were alone again, Tu said, "I will assist you as you have asked. I will arrange for you to speak with certain of my associates in Peking who will tell you things that will aid you in your quest. Then you and I will be done with this matter. You will not bother me again concerning it. Understand?"

I did understand. "*Shi* — *Yes*. We will be done with one another, Master Tu." I bowed my head briefly as my sign of respect.

CHAPTER 59

THE PRESENT

KANJI SAT CROSSED-LEGGED ON THE floor of his borrowed hut. He wore only a thin loincloth. He had covered his entire body with whale oil. A burning charcoal brazier provided minimal illumination and some warmth.

He had already completed practicing his *Aikido* martial art form and had finished his religious rituals. Now he thought about what he wanted to achieve while he remained in Shanghai.

He considered his goals: to identify Matsuko's killer; to take vengeance against that person; and, to restore and protect the reputation of Matsuko and her ancestors.

Kanji was disturbed by what he had observed about Matsuko during his trips to Shanghai. He'd watched her gradually, over three years, drift away from the Code of Bushido into a life of disrespect for her culture and into a morass of wantonness.

She had defiled the Bushido Code, to which she had sworn eternal fidelity, and she had become a drug addict. Almost as bad, she had fraternized with women as well as with men, and, to make this matter worse, she had fraternized with both Chinese and Japanese women and men.

Kanji bowed his head and closed his eyes. After a few minutes, he looked up and stared straight ahead. He had come to the conclusion, to his chagrin, that Matsuko, just as he had predicted and warned her, had willfully turned her back on the young woman she'd been when she lived in Peking at her father's home, before the time when she arrived in Shanghai.

This did not occur by chance, he thought. *Matsuko had been lured to Shanghai, then corrupted.*

Someone would have to pay for seducing Matsuko into this decadent life, leading her away from the Code of Bushido, and causing her to bring shame upon her father, her ancestors, and the Emperor.

He would avenge Matsuko's destruction and death, he thought, *and would bring death to the person who had led her away from Peking and away from the Code of Bushido.*

CHAPTER 60

DAY FOUR OF THE INVESTIGATION

RETURNED HOME FROM TU'S HOUSE. I had some things to do before I would fly to Peking. I attached Bik to her leash, hopped onto the electric trolley with her in tow, and rode out to the French Concession to see Elder Brother.

"Nice surprise," Sun-yu said, as I entered his office. "Sit," he said, motioning me toward the sofa. "We will have cigarettes and a drink."

I settled onto the sofa.

As he started to leave the room to get our drinks, Sun-yu leaned over and patted Bik's head. As he straightened up, he said, "Remember what I told you. If you ever tire of keeping her, my kids would love to have Bik become their dog."

I chuckled. "I'll remember, but don't expect me to tire of her. I won't give her up. She brings great joy to my otherwise ordinary life. Besides," I added, "Mei-hua has told me the same thing, that she'll take Bik should I tire of her. I wouldn't want to have to choose between the two of you if I were giving up this four-legged young lady."

Sun-yu soon returned carrying two bottles of *Ken Kee* beer.

He handed one to me. We clinked bottles for good *joss*. He lit our cigarettes.

"Okay, Younger Brother. How I can help you?"

"Is it that obvious?"

"*Ayeeyah!*" Elder Brother smiled and nodded. "You come here unannounced, in the middle of the day? Two things you rarely have ever done? So, *shi — yes*, it's that obvious. How can I help you?"

"I have to take a trip as part of the murder investigation I told you about. I'll be gone overnight. Will you keep Bik for me until I'm back late tomorrow?"

"Of course. Where are you going?"

"Peking. As a result of my meeting with Big-Eared Tu earlier today."

"Ah! A meeting with Tu. I'm impressed." Sun-yu nodded. "On a different subject," he said, "how is your cover-story article coming for the Round-Eyes woman?"

I shrugged. "I've barely started it. I don't really have time to deal with it. Besides, it's only a cover story, a decoy. I've written just enough and have given that to the Round-Eyes woman to make the cover story seem true to her and to anyone asking her about me. I don't intend to finish it. I don't see any reason to.

"I'll either solve the case and won't need the cover story anymore or I won't solve it in time, in which case the cover story won't help me. Either way, my article won't be relevant at that time as a cover story."

I stood to leave, handing my empty beer bottle to Sun-yu. "See you soon."

I knelt and patted Bik on her head. "I'll miss you, girl."

As I left Sun-yu and stepped out onto the sidewalk, two KMT soldiers suddenly appeared and walked up to me. They moved in close. I was startled by their presence.

"*Ayeeyah!* What do you—"

"*Qing — Please.* Be quiet and come with us. Don't give us any trouble if you know what's good for you."

They marched me over to a jeep and sat me in the back seat with one of them on either side of me. A third soldier drove.

We rode away from the French Concession, across the Garden Bridge, back into the Settlement. When we neared the Bund, the jeep turned north. We drove for another two kilometers or so until we came to a KMT army base. I then was escorted to a house that was occupied by the military.

Outside, near the house's porch, KMT officers stood around smoking cigarettes and talking. A small group of other officers sat at a square table and were setting up to play *mah jong* as we approached them.

The officer escorting me halted as he watched one of the seated officers dump ivory *mah jong* tiles onto the board. Then the officer nodded for me to walk on. Nobody seemed to notice me as I was escorted past the *mah jong* players, up the steps into the house.

∞ ∞ ∞

"Do you know who I am, Mr. Ling?" the colonel, in whose office I was seated, said.

I shook my head. "No, but I can guess."

"*Wǒ jiao Colonel Wu — My name is Colonel Wu.* You have been romantically involved with my daughter for more than one year. That is over. As of now, you will cease all relations with her."

"And if I don't?"

"*Ayeeyah! — Be careful!* I am a powerful man, Mr. Ling. Do not try my patience or test my willingness to cause you harm. This is wartime. Many things can happen to someone in wartime, even to you. No one would ever know or care."

"What if Mei-hua doesn't want me to agree to end our relationship?"

"She is not your concern. I will deal with her."

How wrong he was. Of course Mei-hua was my concern. My only concern in this matter, but I would not say that to him under these conditions.

I had no intention of complying with his order, but I also knew I had to get away from here and go to the airport. Time was slipping away from me. I decided to mislead and appease him.

"*Maskee — No problem.* I'm not looking for trouble, Colonel. I know when I'm beaten. I have no desire to disappear or have anything happen to me. But I have one condition. I'll talk to Mei-hua and end our relationship. Me. Not you."

He remained silent and seemed to think this over. He nodded, then said, "You will not mention our conversation to Mei-hua."

He waited until I nodded my agreement, then said, "My men will return you to your office now. I assume you are not a fool, that I can rely on you, that you will heed my warning."

I nodded again.

CHAPTER 61

DAY FOUR OF THE INVESTIGATION

STILL HAD SOME TIME BEFORE leaving for Peking, so I decided to make one more stop before I left for the airport and for my flight.

I rode a taxi over to the Cathay Hotel. I would try to find some Tower Club employees who would talk to me about the Yellow Swan. I was curious to know if, when she was at her job there, she'd caused conflicting responses among her colleagues, as she'd done at the after-hours clubs she frequented.

I walked into the lobby and stepped into the first available lift. I rode it to the ninth floor. As I stepped out, to my dismay, I faced Inspector Detective Harue, who stood in front of the lift. He appeared to be waiting to ride it down to the lobby.

Harue frowned when he saw me. "What are you doing here?" he said.

I noticed that his hand moved to the butt of his large pistol as he spoke to me.

I was stumped and couldn't quickly respond. I knew that I likely would be arrested by Harue if he did not like my answer. That would prevent me from going to Peking, which would be a disaster. Then the answer came to me.

"When I was here the other day," I said, "when we ran into each other in the lobby, I lost my billfold. I wanted to see if anyone found it and turned it in. I was just going to look for some pageboys or other hotel employees to ask."

Harue squinted, but said nothing. I didn't expect him to believe me, but perhaps the possibility I was telling him the truth would head-off a problem for me.

"Did anyone find it?" he finally said.

"I don't know. I haven't asked yet since I just arrived."

"*Hai!* Did you inquire at the front desk?" Harue said.

"No one has turned it in down there," I lied.

"I could arrest you. Why shouldn't I?"

"Because what I just told you is true. I haven't done anything to justify arrest. I've heeded your warning."

Harue slightly shook his head, but smiled a tiny smile.

"Fortunately for you I have more important things to do right now than arrest you and spend my valuable time filling out forms at the station house. This is your lucky day."

I nodded.

Harue pushed the button and called the lift back. The last I saw of him was Harue glaring at me as the doors closed between us.

I walked around the ninth floor, but did not see anyone to talk to. The doors to the Tower Club were locked. I looked at my wristwatch, then headed home to pick up my valise and then go straight to the airport.

As Inspector Detective Harue stepped out of the lift when it reached the lobby, he thought, *Let the foolish PI look for the Yellow Swan's killer if he wants. He doesn't matter to my mission.*

The incident has now been set in motion and cannot be stopped. Soon it will not matter who murdered the Yellow Swan. It will only matter who we say murdered her.

CHAPTER 62

DAY FOUR OF THE INVESTIGATION

Chief Inspector Chapman banged the bowl of his pipe against his ash tray much harder than he'd intended, scuffing the briar and scattering black ashes over the top of his desk.

He was furious. Sun-jin had not returned his calls.

Chapman picked up his desk telephone and called the duty sergeant. "Send a constable up to see me," he said.

When the uniformed policeman arrived, Chapman said, "Go to the office and home of Ling Sun-jin. See if he's at either place. He's not answering his telephone. If he's there, bring him to me. If he's not there, see if you can find out where he is. Call me in either case before you return to the station house."

When the constable telephoned and reported that Sun-jin was not at either place and that no one knew where he was, Chapman decided to visit Sun-jin's gangster brother. He would squeeze the information from him.

⬦

"Good afternoon, Chief Inspector," Sun-yu said. "Welcome to my humble place of business."

They were out in the nightclub entertaining area, not back in Sun-yu's office. Chapman looked around. The cavernous room was dimly lighted, with only a few scattered table lamps turned on.

I wonder if this is as it would be in the evening when open for business, he thought.

Chapman had never been in a nightclub at night when it was doing business. He'd been in nightclubs only during the day when the establishments were closed, and he was, as a young inspector detective, investigating a crime.

He paused and instinctively inhaled deeply, recalling from deep within his reptilian brain's memory the blended aroma of some odor from long ago. The entertaining room was redolent of stale beer, disinfectant, furtive sex, stale cigarette smoke, and human sweat.

"I'm looking for Sun-jin," Chapman said. "Do you know where he is?"

"Yes and no. I know he's not in Shanghai right now, but I don't know where he's gone. He didn't tell me," Sun-yu lied.

Chapman's neck and face reddened. "What kind of answer is that? That's no help. How do you know he's not in Shanghai?"

"It's the best I can do, Chief Inspector. I just know he left his dog with me and said he'd pick her up when he returns tomorrow."

Chapman frowned.

"I do have a thought, however, that might help you, Chief Inspector."

"Go on."

"His trip must have something to do with some case he's working on because he said he has no time to waste, that he had to leave Shanghai immediately."

"Did he say what kind of case it was?

"I asked, but he wouldn't tell me. He merely said that time was running out and so he had to take a chance and make the trip."

"When he returns for his dog," Chapman said, "tell Sun-jin to call me immediately. And tell him, too, I said he was right. Time has almost run out for him."

CHAPTER 63

DAY FIVE OF THE INVESTIGATION

I RETURNED THE NEXT MORNING FROM my trip to Peking and went directly to Sun-yu's home to retrieve Bik. Judging by her furiously wagging tail when she saw me, and her insistent snout she pushed into my calf as I talked with Elder Brother and his wife, I would say Bik missed me. The feeling was mutual.

"Your old boss came to see me about you," Sun-yu said. "Wanted to know where you were. I said I didn't know."

"*Xiexie — Thanks.* I did not want him to know before I returned, in case my trip was unsuccessful, in which case I wasn't going to tell him."

"He said you are to call him immediately, that time is running out for you. What did he mean by that?"

"I'll call him," I said.

"He tried to find out if you had told me about your investigation. I played dumb."

"Good."

I left Sun-yu and his wife, and headed home. Once there, I fed Bik, gave her water, then let her loose outside.

I called Chapman, left a coded message, and set up a

meeting. Then I took a taxi to Mei-hua's apartment. I still had an hour before I met with Chapman.

Mei-hua reacted to my description of my coerced meeting with her father as I expected she would.

"*Ayeeyah!* How dare him kidnap and threaten you." She stomped around the room, then turned back to me. Her face and neck were bright red. "You stay out of this now. I'll deal with my father."

I hugged her, then kissed her on the side of her neck. "It can hold for now," I said. "We can decide over the next few days how we should handle your father. I have no intention of complying with his order."

CHAPTER 64

THE PRESENT

KANJI PREPARED HIMSELF, MENTALLY AND physically, to kill the person who had lured Matsuko to Shanghai — Victor Sassoon. He said his ritual prayers, then sharpened the edges of his throwing star and dagger.

He watched Sassoon, to the limited extent he was able to actually see him, for three days and nights, learning Sassoon's travel habits between his luxurious apartment in the Cathay Hotel — the 11th floor penthouse, although Kanji had no way of knowing this as he watched the front entrance from outside — and his office in nearby Sassoon House. Kanji's plan was to ambush and kill the Round-Eyes who had enticed Matsuko into coming to Shanghai, the man who had seduced her into abandoning her righteous Bushido life she'd practiced in Peking.

It did not take long for Kanji to understand he would not be able to confront and attack Sassoon as he traveled between his residential venue and office. Sassoon was not a man who casually drifted around the city, making himself vulnerable to attack. He traveled with bodyguards.

Kanji thought about this. The only Asians who seemed

to have access to Sassoon were those who were part of his personal or business group — people such as his comprador — the Celestial, Chen Bao. Unknown Asians, who occasionally approached Sassoon, were routinely confronted by his bodyguards, and were quickly shunted away.

Kanji needed a new plan.

He saw his opportunity that same afternoon and formulated his plan to take advantage of it.

CHAPTER 65

DAY FIVE OF THE INVESTIGATION

C HIEF INSPECTOR CHAPMAN AND I sat down across from one another at the Willow Pattern Tea House. I could see from the frown frozen on his face that he was not happy with me.

"I specifically told you to keep in touch with me, to keep me up to date on your progress," he said. "You ignored me yesterday and did not return my telephone calls."

"That couldn't be helped, sir. I was not in Shanghai. I didn't know you called."

"You need to hire a secretary. No one knew where you were or what you were doing."

"It's supposed to be that way, Chief Inspector. That was your order to me. Secrecy, sir."

"Not concerning me, it wasn't." Chapman sighed and slowly shook his head. "All right, Old Boy, let's forget that. Tell me then. What were you up to in Peking?"

"I had leads to follow. I went to Peking to follow them. Now I'm back. The time you might think was lost, was not wasted," I said. "I can assure you of that."

"Are you going to tell me about it?"

"No, sir, not yet. I have to see if the information is reliable. Then I'll tell you."

"Rubbish! Tell me now. You can modify your statement later, if necessary."

"No, sir. Sorry to seem stubborn, but I won't tell you yet. You have to trust me on this."

"Sun-jin, you work for me, remember?"

I said nothing. I looked hard into the chief inspector's eyes until he broke-off our mutual stares.

"All right," he said, apparently resigned to my stubborn position. "Have it your way, but don't forget that time is running out for Shanghai."

"I know that, sir," I said. "I'm always aware of that."

"And time is running out for you, too," he added.

CHAPTER 66

THE PRESENT

HORSE RACING IN SHANGHAI — or, more accurately, what is locally called China Pony Racing — is promoted by the Shanghai Race Club, a private, elite organization having a club house which features a clock-tower known among the Round-Eyes as Big Bertie.

The Race Club imports ponies from the Mongolian plains, then sells the ponies to its members to help financially sustain the club. The Race Course, along with the Shanghai Club located at No. 2, The Bund, is a center of British-expat social and business life.

The Race Course opened in 1934 at the junction of Nanking and Bubbling Well Roads in the International Settlement. Beginning that year, and for each year thereafter, Victor Sassoon rented a private outdoor box each racing season from which he and his guests watched the races, as they were served food and drink by Chinese attendants.

The first weeks of May and November (Saturday to Saturday, inclusive) brought the popular spring and autumn race meets each year. Everyone who was anyone in Round-Eyes racing or in Shanghai's western-based society attended.

Sassoon, Comprador Chen Bao (who, as a Chinese, was only permitted to sit in Sassoon's box because he was Sassoon's comprador), and Sassoon's former mistress, Mickey Hahn, had come this day to the Race Course to enjoy the opening of the May races and to see Sassoon's two new ponies run. For this occasion, all the British attendees of these premier races dressed specially: the British ladies wore long-sleeve gloves and fancy hats, while the men wore grey top hats and fancy waist coats. Neither Sassoon nor his guests dressed so elaborately.

One of the anomalies of Shanghai's treaty-caste system was that it permitted Japanese residents and visitors to attend functions and visit places that native Chinese, except under special circumstances, were not permitted to attend or visit. The Race Course was one such facility.

Kanji was aware of this bias, having been apprised of local customs by his Shanghai Yakuza brother. He also knew that Sassoon had two entries in Saturday's races since the *North-China Daily News* had reported, three days before, that Sassoon had thrown a lavish party at the Cathay Hotel to welcome the start of the new racing season and to celebrate the entry of his new ponies in the first day's events.

To ready himself for his visit to the Race Course, to ready himself to confront and assassinate Sassoon, Kanji purchased a linen, Western-style business suit, a necktie, and western-style black shoes.

He prepared his dagger that Saturday morning, ritually honing its blade to razor sharpness, then rubbing the entire blade with the venom of the Puffer fish, before sheathing the weapon in a thin oil cloth and placing this ensemble within his jacket in his left inside pocket. The oil cloth would protect Kanji's hand from an accidental, deadly scratch when he reached inside his jacket to extract his weapon.

The grandstand was crowded. It always was on the first day of the racing season. Kanji stood behind the last row of seats, away from the racing infield. He raised his small, monocular spy glass to his eye and surveyed the crowd, looking for Victor Sassoon. He soon found him, seated in his private box with two other people, one a Celestial man and one a Round-Eyes Occidental woman.

Kanji walked over toward Sassoon. The bodyguards glanced at him, saw he was Japanese, not Chinese, and watched him with suspicious eyes, but made no attempt to stop him.

Kanji remained invisible except to Comprador Chen Bao, who warily looked up at Kanji as he suddenly entered the private box.

Kanji quickly, before anyone could react, stepped close to Sassoon, reached into his jacket pocket and pulled out the dagger, letting the oil cloth drop to the ground as he stepped in closer.

As Kanji raised his arm to stab Sassoon, Chen Bao leaped from his seat, grabbed Kanji's striking arm, and pushed Kanji aside, saving the taipan.

Kanji staggered aside, his arm falling in its natural arc as he did so. The knife barely scratched Chen Bao's out-stretched hand.

Chen Bao screamed as he felt the knife cut his skin.

Although he had no way of knowing it, Chen Bao had only minutes to live before the Puffer fish poison would shut down his respiratory system, killing him.

Confusion reigned. People nearby screamed in fear. A crowd surrounded Chen Bao, who laid curled on the floor of the box, his breath labored, foam oozing from his mouth and nose.

Kanji used the cover of this confusion to ease himself away from Sassoon's box and away from the Race Course.

The police arrived within thirty minutes. Out of deference to Sassoon's societal rank, they did not question him at the Race Course. Instead, they accompanied him to his office at Sassoon House to ask him questions.

"Sir Victor," the SMP inspector detective said, "you told the constable that the man who entered your box was Japanese, not Chinese?"

"Correct." Sassoon puffed a cigar.

"Ever seen him before, Taipan?"

Sassoon shook his head.

"Any idea why he would want to harm you?"

"He wouldn't," Sassoon said. "But the man who hired him would."

The inspector detective frowned. He wished the taipan would be more direct in his answers, not require him to pull the answers from him, question by question.

"Who would that be, Sir Victor?"

"Former SMP Inspector Detective Ling Sun-jin," Sassoon said.

"Why would he want to do that, sir?"

"For revenge," Sassoon said. "I cost him his job with the Special Branch. Now he's out working on his own as a private investigator."

"How long ago was that, sir, that you cost him his job?"

"More than a year ago. Almost two."

"You think he still cares enough after all this time to want to kill you?

"I know he does. He came to see me recently to ask for my help with a case he's working on. I turned him down and reminded him I was the bloke who caused him to be dismissed from the SMP.

"Now he's decided it was time to avenge himself. He hired that Japanese person to assassinate me."

The inspector detective raised an eyebrow, but did not comment on Sassoon's conclusion. He turned to the constable standing behind him.

"Pick up Ling Sun-jin and bring him to the station house."

CHAPTER 67

DAY FIVE OF THE INVESTIGATION

I WAS IN MY OFFICE WHEN someone banged on my door. As always, I recognized the authority of the knock. The cops were here. When I opened the door, I faced two uniform constables. They stepped in without asking permission.

"Come with us, Ling Sun-jin. The boss wants to see you. Don't give us no trouble 'cause we'd be glad to accommodate you should you be wantin' a beatin'."

I raised my palms in surrender. "*Ayeeyah!* You won't have any problem from me, Constables," I said. "Let's go see your boss."

"Why'd you want to kill Sir Victor?" said the SMP inspector detective I'd never met before. We sat in his office.

"I didn't," I said. "Did someone try to kill him?"

"You know someone did. In fact, you did, using your hired Jap."

"I don't know anything about it," I said. "I don't have a Jap, hired or otherwise. Just a dog."

"Why'd you go see Sir Victor before the attempt on his life?"

"*Ayeeyah!* I had questions about a case I'm working on. I asked one question. He answered it. I tried to ask other questions. He refused to answer them, so I left. End of story."

"Did it anger you he wouldn't answer your other questions?"

"I expected that, but wanted to be sure, so I tried anyway."

"Anything else happen?"

"He threatened to sue me if I wrote about him in my newspaper article."

"Did that anger you?"

"Not at all. I never intended to include him in my story."

"That's the second time he's gone against you. We know all about how he got you fired from the SMP. Does that still anger you?"

"*Maskee — Not a problem.* Never did. It's ancient history. It doesn't matter anymore."

"Were you at the Race Course today?"

"No."

"Where were you this afternoon?"

"In my office, working. Same place your constables found me."

"Can you prove it? Anyone see you?"

I shook my head. "Just my dog."

"You're lucky we don't have more to hold you on. You can go for now." He pointed his finger at me. "You know the drill. Stay clear of Sir Victor. If he files a complaint against you, it will not go well for you."

I left the SMP station house. I wasn't worried about Sassoon filing a formal complaint against me. I *was* worried about the time I just lost being questioned by the cops. I could not afford a repeat of that.

CHAPTER 68

THE PRESENT

JMP INSPECTOR DETECTIVE HARUE IMPATIENTLY stood on the wharf where the Whangpoo River and Soochow Creek came together, and waited until the general representing the Kwantung army indicated he could speak. Harue's right foot stopped beating the slow tattoo it had tapped as he'd bided his time.

The general looked at Harue. "Speak now," he said. "Tell me, Inspector Detective, when will I have sufficient information from you concerning the murder of the singer so I can act?"

Harue squared his shoulders. "Ah, General, I expect to complete my investigation in two or three days. I will then give you the grounds you need to declare an international incident involving our murdered national."

The general nodded, but said nothing.

Harue believed he was the most important cog in this year's provocation since it would be him — and him alone — who would deliver the pretext for the Kwantung army, air corps, and navy to shell and occupy parts of Shanghai.

"Your information must be compelling," the general said. "The entire world is watching and will be judging us."

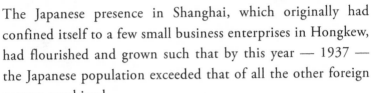

The Japanese presence in Shanghai, which originally had confined itself to a few small business enterprises in Hongkew, had flourished and grown such that by this year — 1937 — the Japanese population exceeded that of all the other foreign powers combined.

In 1934, Japan declared Shanghai to be its protectorate, and warned all the other foreign powers located there (the United States, France, and Britain, among other chief powers) to keep their hands off Shanghai. Of course, this pronouncement was ignored except in seemingly harmless ways.

Although the Japanese community in Shanghai remained nominally under the control of the Shanghai Municipal Council, in fact, Little Tokyo (as Hongkew was known among everyone in Shanghai except the Japanese) was run by the Kwantung army by virtue of treaty rights granted to it after the *January 28 [1932] Incident.*

The Japanese, who had said that the January 28 war with China would be over in a matter of hours, were embarrassed and angry that combat in Chapei took six weeks to resolve. The Kwantung was itching for another fight with the KMT to prove that the Kwantung was superior to China's defense forces. The death of their national, the Yellow Swan, promised to provide just such an opportunity.

"It is my expectation we will begin our bombardment and then our troop advance on Chapei within three days from now," the general said to Harue. "Will you have the information I need before then?"

Harue threw back his shoulders and placed his hand on the hilt of his sword. "I expect to, General. Yes, I certainly will." He beamed with pride.

Harue left the general and walked toward the electric trolley to ride back to JMP headquarters. As he walked, he could see hints of the coming short war about to be visited upon the foolish Celestials and the western Round-Eyes in Shanghai. Groups of Kwantung soldiers in brown uniforms stood along the wharves, rifles hooked casually on their shoulders. Others strutted over the piers, some within Harue's earshot, engaging in verbal saber-rattling.

As he looked down toward the mouth of the Whangpoo River, toward the distant Yangtze River Basin, Harue saw two dozen gunboats anchored there, all crowded with Kwantung soldiers.

He smiled and thought, *It is time for me to complete my investigation and provide the general with the means to declare an international incident.*

CHAPTER 69

THE PRESENT

"IT IS NOT SAFE FOR you to visit me in my encampment, Mei-hua. You have many enemies in the army who know you by sight," Wu Lin-feng said.

"I am not worried, Father. I am able to take care of myself." She paused and took a deep breath. She'd refused his offer to sit, and now paced the floor of his office.

"Don't you really mean it is not safe for your promotion chances for me to be seen at headquarters?" Mei-hua paused, waiting for his answer that did not come. "Am I wrong, Father?"

Lin-feng sighed. "Yes, that, too, Mei-hua. . . . That, too." He returned to his desk and sat. He lifted his foot, struck a wooden match against the sole of his boot, put the flame to the end of his cigarette, and drew hard on the tobacco.

Mei-hua walked over to the front of the desk, placed both her palms on the desktop, and leaned in toward her father.

Lin-feng sighed. "I know why you've come here, Mei-hua. I will not change my mind about the disgraced policeman. Don't waste our time by continuing to try to persuade me to do so or by threatening me again. That has not worked for you in the past and will not work now."

"No threats, Father. Just a clear statement of fact. You should listen carefully to what I have to say."

"And that is?" Lin-feng said. He stiffened his shoulders in anticipation of what he expected to hear.

"I have no intention of ending my relationship with Sun-jin. And if any harm comes to him, you never will see me or hear from me again. Am I clear?"

CHAPTER 70

THE PRESENT

KANJI AND HIS YAKUZA BROTHER sat in Kanji's hut, talking. They finished the rice they'd been eating and put the empty bowls aside. Kanji filled his brother's cup and his own with warm Saki.

"You are sure, Brother?" Kanji said. "The Celestial you've been watching for me is writing a story about Matsuko for a Round-Eyes named Emily Hahn?"

"*Hai!* I'm sure, Kanji-san."

"Who is this Emily Hahn person?"

"She is known as Mickey, not by her given name, Emily. Both are strange names, aren't they?" he said.

"She is a newspaper reporter for the *North-China Daily News*, except she doesn't write about news events. She writes about Celestials and about Round-Eyes. About society people and their decadent lives. The Round-Eyes call her writing, Profiles."

Kanji frowned. "What does she have to do with the disgraced, former inspector detective?"

"Our brothers who work inside that newspaper's office tell me it is common knowledge he is writing a story about

Matsuko-san, referring to her in the early part of the story he has already given to the Hahn woman as *the Yellow Swan*. They also say the Hahn woman is interested in printing whatever he can find out about Matsuko-san, whatever he puts into his Profile of her."

Kanji gulped down the balance of his drink and poured himself another. His face darkened.

"What kind of story is he writing about Matsuko-san?" he asked.

"No one knows, but how could this possibly be good, my brother?"

Kanji was alone now. His Yakuza brother had left him. Kanji considered what he had learned from him.

He would assume the worst concerning the story being written by the former policeman.

The story would surely defame Matsuko. It would probably refer to her as *the Yellow Swan*, rather than refer to her by her given and family names, without respect for her, her family, and her ancestors. It might also describe the decadent life she'd taken on since coming to Shanghai, thereby further shaming her father and ancestors.

Kanji thought, *My path is clear. I cannot allow this to happen. I will not permit this stain upon her family and ancestors to occur. I will stop the Profile before it is written and printed in the newspaper.*

To achieve this, Kanji decided, he would kill the disgraced policeman before he could finish writing the story.

CHAPTER 71

THE PRESENT

Kanji finished honing the point of the pencil-thin, short, bamboo stick until its end was as sharp as a bone sewing needle. He would use this weapon to kill the former policeman, driving the needle into his ear or nostril until it pierced his brain.

Kanji loved this weapon. It was easily concealed in the sleeve of his shirt-top, ready to be dropped into his waiting palm with the flick of his wrist.

Kanji smiled, recalling how inept he'd been with this weapon when his *Aikido* tutor first introduced him to it. In his morning drills, with a blunt-stick substitute having a rubber tip, Kanji had stabbed his bobbing tutor in the side of his head, in his shoulder once, along the top of his scalp another time, and once in his forehead. Within three weeks, however, as the result of daily drills, Kanji had become a skilled, deadly practitioner of the bamboo-stick weapon, and could accurately force it up his opponents nostril into his brain or plunge it through his target's ear drum into his brain, both with deadly accuracy and consistency, with no misplaced thrusts.

3:00 a.m. Kanji easily picked the flimsy lock securing the building's entrance door, and silently made his way up the stairs to Sun-jin's fourth-floor apartment. The building was silent.

He saw no light under Sun-jin's door. He put his ear against the wood and listened. The apartment was silent. He pulled his lock-picking tools from his belt and began working on the door's only lock.

Inside Sun-jin's apartment, Bik suddenly opened her eyes, lifted her head from her crossed front paws, then stood up and faced toward the living room and the apartment's entrance door. She listened, her ears extended straight up.

She growled.

She walked quickly into the living room, stopping at the entrance door. She listened for a few seconds, then turned and trotted back to the bedroom.

Bik listened again, then growled again, louder this time. She turned her head toward the sleeping Sun-jin, then back toward the living room.

Sun-jin briefly opened his eyes and looked at Bik, who stood by the bed, facing the living room.

"Go back to sleep, girl. It's probably the night-soil collector you heard." Sun-jin rolled over on his side and drifted off.

Bik growled again, louder and more insistently this time. She trotted into the living room.

She stopped near the entrance door as it began to slowly open. She turned and ran back into the bedroom.

Kanji opened the apartment's door, then stood still and listened before stepping inside.

He drew out his short-bladed knife to use on the ex-policeman's dog he had seen several times when he followed Sun-jin home. The blade was coated with a poison that would immediately paralyze and silence the animal, leaving Kanji free to deal with Sun-jin.

He looked around. He did not see or hear the dog, *So maybe,* he thought, *the animal is asleep and had not heard him enter the apartment. In that case, he would not be bothered silencing it.* He returned the knife to his belt. He would kill the ex-policeman, then kill the dog if necessary.

He stepped into the living room and silently walked toward the bedroom's entrance. The door to the room was open.

He flicked his wrist, letting the bamboo weapon slide from his sleeve into his waiting palm as he stepped into the darkened bedroom. He paused inside the doorway to allow his eyes to adjust. He heard a low growl from across the darkened room.

Kanji took two steps toward the bed.

He was grabbed by the shoulder from behind.

He spun around toward the open door he'd just passed through.

As Kanji faced the bedroom's entryway, Sun-jin lowered himself into a classic *Shaolin* martial arts attack position, spun once, and kicked Kanji in the chest. Kanji stumbled backward before he gained purchase.

Bik ran over to Kanji and bit his leg, holding him in her tight jaws, violently shaking her head from side-to-side, causing her teeth to sink in more deeply.

Kanji struggled to grab his short knife to finish off the dog. He warily watched as Sun-jin cautiously advanced on him.

Kanji chose to defend himself against the ex-policeman, to let the dog live for now.

Kanji spun as rapidly as he could, lifting his throbbing leg and the dog into the air as he did so. The dog let go of Kanji and skidded away, but turned back quickly. She ran toward Kanji, growling as she closed in on him, her fangs bared.

Kanji rushed toward Sun-jin, his bamboo weapon held in one hand in front of him, ready to strike. His short-bladed knife was now in his other hand.

As he approached Sun-jin, Kanji realized the ex-policeman held a pistol, the barrel of which was pointed at his chest. Kanji pulled himself to a quick halt, keeping his eyes on Sun-jin.

He saw the ex-policeman smile as he prepared to pull the trigger.

Kanji quickly looked around to find a means to escape. His eyes settled on the dog. It was a foot away, growling, and crouched now, ready to spring again.

Before the animal could act, Kanji took one step toward it, leaned over and scooped it up, holding the dog by her throat, his arm extended out and away from his body.

In one fluid motion, Kanji threw the dog into Sun-jin's face.

Sun-jin reflexively lurched sideways, moving his weapon's aim away from Kanji's chest. He fired the shot into the ceiling.

As Sun-jin reacted to the dog in his face and to his misfire, Kanji rushed past him, down the stairs, and out the building.

He would try again, he thought, as he made his escape.

I sat on the side of my bed, my bare feet flat on the cold floor. Bik laid on her back next to my feet. She occasionally let out a forlorn sound, softly moaning. I had checked her and decided she had no injuries. Her eyes stayed fastened on me.

"*Who was that?*" I wondered. "*Why would this man want to kill me?*"

I bent over, scratched Bik's stomach for a few seconds, then stood up.

I walked around my apartment. Bik trailed along close behind me.

I didn't see any sign that the intruder had stolen anything from my living room or kitchen before he entered my bedroom. I also didn't see any evidence he'd searched my drawers or my wardrobe, so I ruled out burglary as the motive for the intruder being in my home.

I doubted he'd been surprised to find me in the bedroom at 3:00 a.m., so I decided he had come to kill me, but, thanks to Bik's warning and assistance, had failed.

I assumed this attempt on my life somehow related to my investigation, but why and how I couldn't figure out at the moment.

I knew there was likely only one person who would know what was behind the attempt on my life, one person who might help me by telling me why I was attacked and who had been behind it.

At daybreak, I would again go visit Big-Eared Tu, notwithstanding our agreement that I would not bother him again concerning the investigation. This was different now, I decided. Tu would understand.

CHAPTER 72

DAY SIX OF THE INVESTIGATION

ARRIVED AT THE ZIG-ZAGGED DRIVEWAY leading to Big-Eared Tu's house just as he walked up the long path ahead of me, heading toward his front door. He carried a songbird cage in his right hand.

Tu, as he'd always been before, was gracious. He agreed to see me even though I had not made an appointment before showing up at his doorstep first thing in the morning, and even though we had agreed not to meet again. He led me into his house. We settled into his Great Room.

"Welcome again to my home, Sun-jin. I assume you are once more going to ask for my help," Tu said, once we finished the expected Tao and Confucian ritualized small talk, in this instance talk about the songbird he'd been carrying when I called out to him before he stepped into his home.

"Yes, Master Tu, I am. Although we agreed before I headed off to Peking that we were finished with one another concerning this matter, it now is urgent that I ask you to set that understanding aside for the time being and give me your help. I hope you will indulge my needs this one more time and will see your way to assist me.

Tu nodded, but committed to nothing. He placed his hands on his lap and intertwined his fingers.

I told Tu everything about my investigation, including details about my conversations with his associates in Peking. Then I told him how someone had tried to kill me the previous evening.

Tu said nothing.

"I believe, Master Tu, that our interests in this matter might now coincide."

"Why would you think that? I am a businessman. You are a disgraced former policeman."

"Because, as you know from our previous meetings, Master Tu, the reason I'm investigating the murder of the Yellow Swan is to head-off a contrived incident likely to be raised by the Kwantung military as an excuse to bombard and invade the city."

Tu said, "That was the same reason as when you first came to me to ask for my assistance. I still fail to see that we have any mutual interest here."

I didn't believe he actually felt that way, but I knew better than to say so. To do that would cause Tu to lose face. Instead, I pressed my argument.

"Your interest, Master Tu, arises precisely because you are a businessman. If the Kwantung uses the Yellow Swan's murder to precipitate an incident, the military action and the combat that will follow surely will harm your business in Shanghai."

Tu rang a bell. We waited silently while a serving coolie entered, poured tea for us, then left the Great Room.

When we were alone again, Tu said, "You are correct. I had already decided that our interests do coincide in some limited measure, at least they do for the moment."

Tu adjusted the sleeves of his Mandarin gown before looking up at me.

"My business associates, those in Shanghai and the others who met with you in Peking, already informed me early this morning that the warrior who attacked you last evening is named Kanji Gorō. He is a Dwarf Bandit Yakuza."

That gave me pause. *Why would a criminal, Yakuza warrior come from Peking to Shanghai to assassinate me?* I suddenly found myself breathing very quickly.

"Are you certain, Master Tu?"

"Of course I'm certain. This was not a random act. This Yakuza came to Shanghai on a mission, on his own mission, I am informed by my associates, not for a Yakuza assignment."

"Why would this Yakuza want to kill me?"

"He also tried to kill Taipan Sassoon at the Race Course on Saturday, but failed. The Taipan's comprador, Chen Bao, died protecting his taipan."

That puzzled me. "But why us?"

"This Yakuza had been the Yellow Swan's lover when she lived in Peking," Tu said. "She had been so then, but no longer remained his lover once she arrived in Shanghai.

"Before that, she was a loyal and committed follower of the Way of Bushido. Kanji Gorō, in addition to being Yakuza, also is Bushido."

I was beginning to see the link.

"My associates also tell me that this Yakuza arranged to have her watched in Shanghai. His Shanghai Yakuza brother reported to Gorō that the Yellow Swan regularly fraternized with generals and some lesser officers in General Chiang's KMT army. She did this to gain information that would assist the Japanese Kwantung."

"Why would that offend Gorō. I should think he would be pleased with that role for her?" I said.

"Perhaps," Tu said, "but perhaps things weren't as they seemed. Perhaps this Yakuza resented her relationship with Celestials more than he welcomed her assistance to the Kwantung military."

That seems possible.

"Master Tu," I said, "I assume everything you've told me is accurate. But how do I fit in? Why would the Yakuza want to kill me? Was I about to discover something in my investigation that he wanted to remain hidden?"

"Possibly. Perhaps that would have eventually motivated him to kill you, but from his viewpoint, there was a more urgent matter involving you that likely spurred him on to eliminate you now."

"What would that be?"

"You are writing a story about the Yellow Swan for the Round-Eyes American reporter, Mickey Hahn. That's what concerned this Yakuza."

Then I understood. It was obvious now that Tu had led me to the answer. The Yakuza wanted to protect the Yellow Swan's reputation from disclosure by me through my article.

That's ironic, I thought, *since I don't intend to finish and submit the story.*

He also wanted to avenge her ruinous fall from the Way in Shanghai by killing the person who convinced her to come to this city, the person who seduced her into becoming the Yellow Swan. That person, of course, was Victor Sassoon.

"I understand now, Master Tu," I said, offering him my respect by bowing my head.

As I said this, Tu stood up and nodded. Our meeting was over.

I left Tu's home and rode the electric streetcar back to the Bund. From there, I walked to my office.

I thought about what I had learned from Tu. Everything he'd said explained why I had been attacked by the Yakuza. It did not, however, tell me who had killed the Yellow Swan.

Had it been the Yakuza, I wondered, *because he was angry she had forsaken her Bushido principles and had become friendly with Chinese men and women? Had his repulsion for her Shanghai lifestyle overwhelmed his love for her and caused him to brutally murder her?*

I didn't know the answer to that. What I did know was that I had only one day left to solve the murder.

PART FOUR

CHAPTER 73

DAY SIX OF THE INVESTIGATION

EVEN THOUGH TIME WAS SLIPPING away from me, I knew I had to take a deep breath, stop what I'd been doing, and think about and assimilate the information I currently had from my own inquiries, from Elder Brother's triad associates, and from Big-Eared Tu's Peking Green Gang members. The lost time to do this would be justified, I believed, if it helped steer me toward the correct results. If it didn't . . . well, I doubted I would be any worse off than I was now, this late in the week.

I sat at my kitchen table and thought about what I knew about the Yellow Swan.

What did I actually know?

I knew her true name — Matsuko Akasuki.

I also knew that when she still lived in Peking, she'd been an ardent follower of the Way of Bushido, but, having resided in Shanghai for three years, she'd strayed from, or had just rejected altogether, that code for conducting her life.

I knew that her mother, a Chinese woman, had died a mysterious death when Matsuko was seven years old, and that her father, a fervent and vocal Dwarf Bandit nationalist, still lived in Peking, where he worked as a minor diplomat at the Dwarf Bandit's embassy.

I also knew that Kanji Gorō, a member of the Yakuza, had been her lover in Peking. And I knew that Kanji had come to Shanghai to avenge her murder and to restore and protect her reputation.

I'd learned that Matsuko occasionally worked as a flower-seller girl, and was indiscriminate in choosing her customers. I learned, too, that since coming to Shanghai, she had become addicted to cocaine and opium.

From my investigation, I learned that she often was seen in the company of Chinese nationals — especially military officers — as well as Dwarf Bandit nationals, especially military men, living or deployed in Shanghai.

And I learned that she presented the world with two different personalities, depending on where she might be. When she was at a Dwarf Bandit after-hours club, she was much disliked by the people who crossed her path — too often drinking too much, taking opium or cocaine, and being abusive. But when she was at a Chinese after-hours club, she refrained from using drugs, drank little, and remained friendly and respectful.

Matsuko — the Yellow Swan — I concluded, was a contradiction in personalities and behaviors.

But, Ayeeyah, I wondered, where has all this knowledge taken me in my investigation?

CHAPTER 74

THE PRESENT

Inspector Detective Akio Harue stood with Kwantung General Narita Fudo on a wharf projecting out into the Whangpoo River, near the southern end of the Bund. He stared at the twenty-eight gunboats, warships, and troop carriers the general had amassed in anticipation of responding to an incident, real or contrived, involving the murder of the Japanese national, Matsuko Akasuki. What Harue could not see, but had heard rumors concerning, were the many gunboats and other vessels waiting to be called forth from their moorings between Shanghai and the mouth of the Yangtze River Basin, eighty-seven kilometers away.

"*Hai!* I am impressed, General, by the show of force you've amassed," Harue said.

"It is more than a *show* of force, Mr. Policeman. It *is* force. I am ready to teach the Celestials and Round-Eyes a lesson they will not soon forget, once we have all our pieces in place."

"I still am working on my part, General. I will need a few more days, then you can proceed."

"*Hai!* This might not even require an incident occurring in

Shanghai," the general said. "I understand from my colleagues in Peking that such an event is close to occurring there, at a bridge known as the Lugou Bridge — what the Round-Eyes call the Marco Polo Bridge — and that this will give our other forces the basis for attacking Peking."

Harue smiled. He squared his shoulders.

"Should that incident occur before one occurs here, I will use it as the basis for taking action in this city, too," the general said. He lit a *Craven A* cigarette, the most expensive cigarette sold in Shanghai, inhaled it, and then blew out smoke.

"*Hai!* As you see fit, General," Harue said. "I am happy to assist you in your glorious mission in any way I can."

The general dropped his cigarette onto the wharf and crushed it under his boot.

"There is one problem," he said. "It seems the information about troop movements and troop strength in Shanghai we received ten days ago from our contact at our embassy in Peking was misleading.

"We have confirmed that the information he sent us — intelligence he received from someone in Shanghai — significantly underestimated the number of Celestial troops, especially with regard to the Shanghai Volunteer Corps and the Nineteenth Route Army. Our civilian source here in Shanghai misled the embassy, which, in turn, misled us."

"*Hai!* Will that affect your ability to act, General?"

"Not now that we know about it, but it could have. We must find out who passed the incorrect information onto our Peking contact so we can prevent it from happening again."

The general turned and faced his waiting troops again.

"Soon," he said, "very soon, one way or the other, I

will unleash these men, their weapons, and our planes against Chapei. Perhaps even against the Round-Eyes in the International Settlement and French Concession."

CHAPTER 75

DAY SEVEN OF THE INVESTIGATION

I CALLED THE CHIEF INSPECTOR AND arranged to meet with him. Now that my trip to Peking had been successful, I was ready to tell him about it.

We did not meet at the Willow Pattern Tea House as we usually did. For some reason, Chapman did not seem to care at this point if anyone knew I was investigating the murder. I suppose this was because time was running out for us, running out for Shanghai. We met in his office at the SMP station house.

"Time's almost up, Old Boy," Chapman said. "It is now one week. The Japs are poised down by the Bund to strike at any time."

"I know."

The chief inspector squinted at me.

"I need more time to wrap this up," I said. "I'm close to resolving the murder, but I need a little more time."

"I doubt we have more time."

I nodded. "Let me keep going, Chief Inspector. Drop the one-week deadline. I'm very close to finishing this. I might be able to resolve it before the Dwarf Bandits contrive their incident.

"Besides," I said, "since they aren't aware of the deadline you imposed on me, we have nothing to lose by continuing on with the investigation."

The chief inspector reached into his pocket and removed his pipe and tobacco pouch. He remained silent. He clearly was thinking about what I just said.

He filled his pipe, tamped down the tobacco with his stained thumb, then put a match to the bowl.

"All right, Sun-jin, keep going, but with two conditions. You continue to move along as quickly as possible, as if you still are under a deadline, which you are, and you tell me now everything you know about the case.

"Don't hold anything back. I know you well enough from your time with the Special Branch not to think you've told me everything or that you have been completely forthcoming with me, Old Boy.

"Start with your trip to Peking — why you went there, who you met with, and what you learned."

CHAPTER 76

DAY SEVEN OF THE INVESTIGATION

BEFORE I STARTED TALKING, THE chief inspector stood up from behind his desk, walked over to his office door, and closed it. He returned to his desk, sat down, then looked at me again. He drew heavily on his pipe.

"Go ahead," he said. "I'm listening."

I described my trip, touching upon each of the points he just raised.

I told him about my last meeting with Big-Eared Tu, and that Tu had put me in touch with members of the Green Gang in Peking. I described my trip to Peking, and how I learned that Matsuko's father not only was a diplomat for the Dwarf Bandits in Peking, but was a conduit to the Kwantung army for information about troops he'd learned about from the Yellow Swan, while she was living in Shanghai.

"So, the Yellow Swan was a Jap spy, was she?" Chapman said. He narrowed his eyes. "That could explain her murder."

"Yes and no. She was a double agent. It seems she deliberately fed her father inaccurate information about our military the week before she died."

"Why would she do that?"

"Apparently, she'd learned that her father, a crazed nationalist, regretted having married her mother when they were young, and arranged to have her killed when the Yellow Swan was a child."

"I see," Chapman said. He knocked the bowl of his pipe against his ashtray, dislodging black ashes.

I continued. "He also despised the life-style the Yellow Swan succumbed to while she lived here. He believed she not only had shamed him, as her father, but also had shamed their ancestors and the Emperor. He could not, under his Bushido Code, permit her to continue that way.

"He repeatedly tried to have her return to Peking to live, but she refused to do so.

"In the end, the Yellow Swan's father came to Shanghai, confronted her with her misdeeds, and ordered her back to Peking to again embrace the Way of Bushido to redeem herself.

"When she refused to leave Shanghai, he ordered her to perform *Hari Kari*, even giving her a Seppuku knife with which to conduct the ritual suicide."

"Interesting," the chief inspector said. "She obviously did not obey her father, so what happened?"

"Her father, angry and heart-broken, returned alone to Peking. There he allowed his anger to fester and build over several weeks."

"Anything else?" the chief inspector said.

I nodded. "The final straw was when he learned she recently had given him false information concerning Nineteenth Route Army troop movements, information he passed on to the Kwantung in Shanghai, as if it were valid."

"Then what happened?," the chief inspector asked.

"Her father arranged for someone to come to Shanghai to kill her."

"Interesting, Old Boy. And you trust this information?

"I trust that members of the Green Gang would not feed me false information when Big-Eared Tu ordered them to help me."

"Anything else?" Chapman said.

I shook my head.

"How will you use this information to head off an incident?" Chapman asked.

"If you can arrange to have Matsuko's father arrested for murder in Peking, we then can publicize that he caused her death. Hopefully, that public disclosure will embarrass the Kwantung and, therefore, will block any attempt by the Dwarf Bandits to seek an incident based on the Yellow Swan's murder."

The chief inspector said nothing to me. Instead, he picked up his Bakelite telephone and said into it, "I say, Old Girl, get me the chief of police in Peking. Tell them it's urgent."

CHAPTER 77

THE PRESENT

"**M**Y MOTHER AND FATHER," MEI-HUA whispered into my ear as we laid close together in her bed, "have at last agreed to accept you as a former policeman, and to accept that you are a *low faan* — accept you for now, that is."

I smiled a dubious smile.

"I know them well enough to know that they believe time will resolve their concern, that you and I will eventually tire of one another and go our separate ways."

"What do you mean, accept me *for now?*"

Mei-hua laughed. "It means my father said he is too busy dealing with the coming war, and with the Dwarf Bandits, and with Communists in Shanghai, to worry about you. *For now.* After the war, well, that's another matter."

I laughed, too, and shook my head. "*Ayeeyah!* I can accept that." I smiled. "For now."

Mei-hua thought, *If only it will be that easy and that trouble free when the time comes for us to part.*

She put her arm around Sun-jin's shoulder and pulled him in close to her.

CHAPTER 78

JULY 7, 1937

I was at home on the morning of July 7, finishing breakfast, when the news came over the radio that Dwarf Bandit forces in Peking had launched an attack at 2:00 o'clock this morning. The British radio announcer referred to the Dwarf Bandits' intrusion into Peking as the Marco Polo Bridge Incident. Because of the date of the occurrence, July 7, we Chinese refer to this event as the Double-Seven Incident.

According to the radio announcer, earlier the day before, after the Kwantung conducted maneuvers outside Peking, the army discovered that one of its soldiers was missing. The Kwantung accused the Chinese of having kidnapped him, and used this excuse to drop bombs this morning on Peking and to have thousands of Kwantung troops pour into the city and into other parts of northern China, including Tientsin.

The missing soldier was later discovered in a nearby brothel where he'd been sleeping-off his hangover. But it was too late. The undeclared war — what the Dwarf Bandits gleefully referred to as the Greater East Asian War — had started.

CHAPTER 79

THE INVESTIGATION: ONE WEEK + ONE DAY
JULY 8, 1937

M EI-HUA AND I WERE EATING breakfast at her apartment when we heard the explosions in the distance. We abruptly looked up at one another, both frowning, but said nothing. We would learn later that these sounds came from bombs being dropped by Dwarf Bandit airplanes over Chapei. They would be the first of many to fall on the Old City.

Bik stood by the window, her front paws on the sill, looking out. She seemed rigid and nervous. Every once in a while she would let out a soft moan, and turn her head to briefly look back at us.

Following the suggestion of the SMP broadcast over British radio to avoid congestion in the streets, Mei-hua and I remained indoors, but discussed all morning what we expected to happen now that Shanghai was being bombed.

Would the fighting spread from Chapei? we wondered. *Would the Dwarf Bandits invade the Settlement and the French Concession, bringing the British, Americans, and French into the new war?*

We certainly hoped so. We could use allies in the coming fight with the Dwarf Bandits.

As the day wore on, our nerves became frayed with dreaded anticipation. I decided to raise a different subject to get our minds off the bombing.

"Are you still a member of the CCP, even though you don't seem to be active?" I asked.

Mei-hua frowned. "*Qing rang? — Excuse me?* Why would you ask that?"

I shrugged. "*Dui bu qi — Sorry.* Just trying to get our minds off the war so we can calm down. Seemed like a good idea. No other reason."

She nodded. "Not formally. I gave up that for my parents' sake."

"What's that mean," I said, "not formally?"

"I still have friends in the Revolution who are active. We talk about it when we get together. That's all. I'm no longer active. I told you that before."

This bothered me. *Mei-hua still supports the Revolution and wants to topple all I believe in — most of what I still believe in. She continues to want to overthrow the rules, laws, and customs I have always believed in.* This did not please the Confucian in me.

Mei-hua reached out and took my hand. "What's really bothering you, Sun-jin? I know you brought this up for some reason, not just to distract us both from the bombing we still can hear."

"All right. I'll tell you," I said. "You're playing a dangerous game, Mei-hua, and I worry that you'll be harmed. Your father was right when he made you recant your previous CCP life in your letter to the *North-China Daily News*. But that's not enough.

"It's likely we are coming into turbulent times, with war all around us. The chaos will present a perfect opportunity for your enemies and for your father's enemies to strike against you, but blame it on the war. You must protect yourself. Start by ceasing your affiliation with your CCP friends."

Mei-hua's eyes narrowed. "I always watch out for myself, Sun-jin. I am not worried, but I understand your concern."

She paused and patted my hand. "I'm careful. I no longer attend meetings or rallies, boycotts or strikes. I have kept a low profile. To the outside world who read my letter, I am a former Communist. That will never change. They will always see me that way, but I now am reformed so I will be safe."

I nodded. I knew she probably believed what she was saying, yet I worried that the coming turbulent times would offer an opportunity for someone to prove her wrong.

CHAPTER 80

THE INVESTIGATION: ONE WEEK + TWO DAYS
JULY 9, 1937

I LEFT THE SANCTUARY OF MEI-HUA'S apartment this morning. I went home. I walked around my neighborhood watching people and observing merchants as they prepared for war. Much had changed in only a few days.

Everyone I encountered has been upended by the news of the Marco Polo Bridge Incident in Peking on July 7, by the invasion and occupation of Peking by the Dwarf Bandits, and by the bombing of the Old City here in Shanghai.

We have all anticipated that Shanghai will be next to be invaded. We just don't know when that will occur, how long it might last, and how ferocious the Dwarf Bandits might be in pursuing their occupation of the city.

———◆———

Chief Inspector Chapman and I met early in the afternoon in his office.

"The Peking police arrested the Yellow Swan's father the day before the Japs invaded Peking," he said. "The man confessed to having arranged with the Dwarf Bandits' Black Dragon Society for the murder of his wife years ago because she was corrupting their daughter.

"He also confessed to using that same secret Society to have his daughter murdered to punish her for abandoning the Way of Bushido, for forsaking the Emperor, and for having shamed him and his ancestors with her disgraceful life-style while living in Shanghai."

"Did he say anything about the Yellow Swan spying for Japan, as we suspected?" I said.

The chief inspector nodded. "Yes." He paused. "Apparently he knew his daughter was a spy for Chiang's army, that she was acting as a double agent against the Kwantung, against the Emperor.

"He said she fed him misleading information the week before her death, information which he innocently passed along to the Kwantung military, not only harming the Emperor's glorious cause, but causing him, as Matsuko's father, irreversible shame.

"He also indicated that as the police arrived to arrest him, he was preparing to take his own life to mitigate his dishonor. The Peking police confiscated his weapon and other ritual paraphernalia he was going to use to kill himself."

That surprised me, but it would explain why he'd had his daughter murdered. Likely it had been the combination of factors described by the chief inspector — his daughter's treachery against the Emperor and the Imperial state, her spying for the enemy, the shame she brought upon the family by causing her father to pass along unreliable intelligence,, and her decadent life style in Shanghai.

I turned the subject to one that was as important to me as the news the chief inspector had just delivered.

"Sir," I said, "may I ask a favor of you?"

The chief inspector's eyes narrowed. "Go on."

"Now that the Yellow Swan case is wrapped up," I said, "would you reconsider your previous position and attempt to have my private investigator's license issued so I can work in the open?"

"No. Your work on the Yellow Swan case keeps you out of prison for your past violations. It does not open new doors for you."

I was disappointed, but not surprised.

"Of course, Sun-jin," the chief inspector said, "if you're discreet going forward as a PI, even if you should happen to carry a pistol without a permit, I cannot arrest you for violating the Municipal Code if I don't know about the violations." He smiled slightly, nodded once, raised his eyebrows, and shrugged his shoulders.

"*Xiexie — Thank you.* I understand, Chief Inspector."

CHAPTER 81

JULY 9, 1937

K ANJI WAS SHOCKED BY THE news his Yakuza brother brought him.

He'd been sitting in the borrowed hut, listening to the explosion of bombs in the distance, and considering a way to successfully kill Victor Sassoon and Sun-jin, when his Yakuza brother entered carrying a copy of *New Bamboo Blossom*, one of Shanghai's Japanese-language newspapers sold in Hongkew.

"Do you know this for sure?" Kanji asked his Yakuza brother, when he'd told Kanji his news. "Matsuko's father murdered her? Why would he do that?"

"The article does not say, my brother. Perhaps he was crazy. Maybe he was a spy for the enemy. Who knows?"

Kanji thought about that. *None of that made sense. He felt shame he had not seen this as a possibility.*

"Will you return to Peking, Kanji-san, now that your mission is ended?"

Kanji considered his answer. *He could stay and complete his mission against the Round-Eyes Sassoon and the newspaper story writer, but what good would that do in light of the damaging information now tainting Matsuko and her ancestors.*

With all the questions raised by her death at the hand of her father, nothing could restore Matsuko's reputation and assuage her ancestors.

Better to complete the one assignment he knew he could succeed at.

He sat alone in the hut.

He knew the path he had to take.

Seppuku. *An honorable ritual death given his failure to fulfill his mission in Shanghai. He had brought shame on himself and on his Yakuza family.*

Seppuku had been banned by law in Japan in 1873, but, as everyone knew, the ritual still occurred when the circumstances called for it. This was one such time.

He would cleanse himself of his failure and would honor his disgraced ancestors. He would honor the *Oyabun* and his Yakuza brothers. He would slice open his stomach and disembowel himself.

Kanji bathed himself and covered his entire body in whale oil.

He thought about Matsuko, and how he had failed her.

Then he stood up and walked over to his weapons' cache. He selected a short bladed dagger — a *tantou* — to use.

CHAPTER 82

JULY 9, 1937

LEFT THE CHIEF INSPECTOR'S OFFICE satisfied that my life as an illicit private investigator had taken a turn for the better, as far as the chief inspector and the SMP were concerned, provided I was discreet in my operations. I could handle that. I wondered, however, how this might turn out if the Dwarf Bandits, as everyone now predicted, would eventually occupy many parts of our city.

Would my business then be confined to the International Settlement and French Concession, since the Kwantung might not risk war with Britain, the United States, and France by attacking their Concession territories?

How would that affect my professional life? Would I be prevented from operating in those parts of Chinese Shanghai that were occupied by the Dwarf Bandits, or would I be allowed to do business there?

Would I be able to engage in espionage against the Dwarf Bandits, using my role as a PI as cover? I was determined to play that role once our city was occupied, as it certainly would be.

CHAPTER 83

AUGUST 9, 1937

THE LOCAL NEWSPAPERS PREDICTED THAT the Yangtze Valley would be the next front in the war between China and the Dwarf Bandits. Specifically, the newspapers argued that since Chiang and his KMT forces could not defeat the Dwarf Bandits without help from other countries, he would engage the enemy in urban Shanghai, hoping that by doing so he would force Britain, France, and the United States to join him against the invaders, once the invasion occurred. Accordingly, Chiang increased his army's presence near Shanghai.

The Dwarf Bandits responded to Chiang's buildup of forces by increasing the number of their troops there.

By August 9, the Dwarf Bandits had forty-six warships and gunboats stationed opposite the Bund, in an area we locals now referred to as Battleship Alley. The armada included its flagship, the *Idzumo Maru*, which was anchored in clear view of the Cathay Hotel.

This afternoon, two Dwarf Bandit soldiers tried to force their way into Shanghai's Aerodrome, located to the west of the city.

They were shot and killed by the Chinese Peace Preservation Corps guards.

The local Dwarf Bandit press called the incident, the "Aerodrome Murders," and then incited the local Dwarf Bandits in Hongkew to riot against us.

Warships in Battleship Alley readied for war. Additional troop-carrying ships arrived from the Yangtze River Basin, and docked in the Whangpoo opposite the Bund.

The gunboats *Seta Maru* and *Kuri Maru* shelled northern Shanghai. Kwantung troops landed in Chapei, driving midget, two-man tanks. Other troops came on foot. The ensuing fighting was fierce.

The Chinese air force unsuccessfully tried to sink the *Idzumo Maru*. The Dwarf Bandit's air force and navy responded by bombing that part of the International Settlement that is not Chapei. This was the first time this had occurred since 1928.

The first bomb that dropped into the Settlement hit the Palace Hotel. Shrapnel from its explosion sprayed the new post office building's clock tower, stopping the clock at 4:27 p.m. Chaos and mayhem followed. Before too long, Shanghai's hospitals were full.

———— ◆ ————

When the shelling and fighting finally ended at sundown, life in Shanghai had changed. Parts of the city outside the Concessions were fully occupied by the Kwantung, with troops pressing close to, and, by their very presence, threatening the entire International Settlement and French Concession. The radio has referred to the carnage as Bloody Saturday.

———— ◆ ————

I now understand that my life as a private investigator will be different from what it has been up to now. I will have to learn to operate within the confines of the Dwarf Bandit's occupation of Shanghai, once that comes, and within the confines of their military's rules and regulations.

I will seek out opportunities to spy against the Dwarf Bandits.

How different things actually will be for me, remain unknown. I have no idea, but I will move forward, practicing my business as an unlicensed, unlawful private investigator and learning to be a spy for my city.

What other choice do I have in these turbulent times?

THE END

PLEASE REVIEW *DEATH OF THE YELLOW SWAN* ON AMAZON

If you enjoyed **DEATH OF THE YELLOW SWAN**, please post a review on Amazon at **www.Amazon.com**. Search for the book review page under my name or under the book's title, **DEATH OF THE YELLOW SWAN**.

DOWNLOAD A FREE COPY *MANDARIN YELLOW*

The first Socrates Cheng mystery
Copy and paste this link into your browser or, if you are reading the page on a tablet or other digital device, click this link to download a free copy:
http://www.stevenmroth.com/FreeBook.aspx

Visit me at www.StevenMRoth.com to see all of my published books and receive information about my upcoming books

STEVEN M. ROTH

www.StevenMRoth.com

Steve, a retired lawyer, has written (i) a three-book mystery series featuring his Chinese/Greek/American private eye, Socrates Cheng, (ii) a two-book thriller/suspense series featuring ex-Navy SEAL, Trace Austin, and, (iii) a two-book mystery series set in 1930s Shanghai, China, featuring ex-cop Sun-jin.

All of Steve's books have a solid and interesting historic and cultural aspect to their plots, and all are well researched and developed to reflect these aspects of Steve's stories. The Socrates Cheng mystery series explores murder within the historical context of Socrates' Chinese heritage (MANDARIN YELLOW), within the historical context of Socrates' Greek heritage (THE MOURNING WOMAN), and in relationship to Socrates' interest in the Civil War and in Robert E. Lee (THE COUNTERFEIT TWIN).

Steve's suspense/thriller series (NO SAFE PLACE and NO PLACE TO HIDE), featuring ex-Navy SEAL Trace Austin, explores the plight of an individual and his family who are innocently caught-up in intrigues involving the abuse of Presidential power and home-grown biological-weapon terrorism in the United States.

Steve's new Shanghai murder mystery series is projected to

comprise five books, and takes place in Shanghai, China, from 1935 until December 7, 1941, when the Japanese occupied and took control of all Shanghai. The first book in the series (DEATH IN THE FLOWERY KINGDOM) involves murder, cultural clashes, and Shanghai's conflicting and confusing ambiance in 1935, all as experienced by Shanghai Municipal Police Inspector-Detective, Sun-jin. The second book in the series (DEATH OF THE YELLOW SWAN) is a fast-paced "who done it" set against the background of the coming invasion of Shanghai by the Japanese.

Steve is currently writing the third Trace Austin suspense/thriller.

More information about Steve's books and other information about him can be found on Steve's web site at **www.StevenMRoth.com**.

Feel free to contact Steve at:
http://www.stevenmroth.com/ContactMe.aspx
Twitter: @StevenMRoth
Facebook: http://tinyurl.com/44c3bsp